To Kidnap
A Princess

by

Ian Ball

2022

Contents

Chapter 1

Princess Anne, looking regal, exits the banqueting hall, pauses at the top of the stairs. She looks smaller than I had expected, though I suspect that is due to the presence of her husband beside her. Captain Mark Phillips, cavalry officer and Olympic showjumper, is six feet two.

Her Royal Highness trots down the stairs and climbs into the waiting car, a maroon Rolls-Royce limousine marked with the royal insignia. Captain Phillips sits on one side of her, her lady in waiting on the other, while her bodyguard occupies the passenger seat. I watch as the driver skilfully manoeuvres the car along the driveway and out into London's busy early evening traffic.

I take a deep breath. I'm ready, waiting, months of planning coming together for just this moment. As the car passes me I rev my engine to avoid stalling, then pull out to follow, driving cautiously so as not to attract attention.

I glance down at my waistcoat for what feels like the fiftieth time. In the left-hand pocket is a snub nosed .38 ready for a quick draw, in the right a snub nosed .34.

I move smoothly through the traffic and draw up behind the royal car. Together we potter along The Strand towards Trafalgar Square, no one suspecting anything of the anonymous white Ford Escort following the royal car.

As we begin to circle the Square I am startled by the wail of a blaring horn as a large van cuts in front of me, in a rush to get somewhere. I slam on the anchors and swerve to the right, manage to stall the engine.

'Shit! Shit! Shit!"

As I crank the key I peer through the traffic. I've lost sight of the royal car.

The car coughs, once, twice, and for a moment I think I've flooded it, then it catches with a plume of black smoke from the exhaust. I press the clutch pedal to the floor, slam the gear stick into first, floor the accelerator and make a tyre-screeching take-off in the direction of the royal car.

I bear left and accelerate hard along The Mall – I know where Princess Anne's car is heading – quickly picking up speed. The engine screams in protest as I hit 40, 50, 60, 70. I'm closing fast, and then in a flash I'm past them and there is clear air between us. I jerk the wheel to the left and brake violently and the royal car almost slams into the back of me as the driver also brakes hard. Our tyres squeal, leaving burnt rubber on the tarmac.

There is a long second of silence, no one moving. The only sound I can hear is my own ragged breathing, my rapid-fire heartbeat pounding in my ears, then I hurl the car door open, step out. This is the moment I've been waiting for, the moment I've been planning for months, the moment when it all comes together.

I run towards the royal car, pull out my pistols, wrench the passenger door open.

Princess Anne looks up at me in surprise. "What's happening? What's going on?" she demands. I can only admire her calm demeanour.

"Come with me," I tell her.

She makes no move to get out. "Why would I do that?"

"I just want you for a couple of days," I plead.

"I don't want to come with you," she says emphatically.

This isn't going the way I had planned it.

"You have to!" I beg, grabbing her arm.

As I try to drag her out, Captain Phillips grabs her other arm, and we have a bizarre tug of war, with the Princess in the middle.

"Please come with me," I beg, but as I speak I see something out the corner of my eye. While Princess Anne has distracted me, her bodyguard has climbed out of the car, drawn his gun.

The black orifice of its barrel stares me in the eye. This could be all over before it begins.

As I slowly turn I see the bodyguard's finger tighten on the trigger.

Click.

Nothing happens.

Nothing happens! His gun has jammed. Saying a silent prayer, I turn and fire my .38. There is an explosion of starlight as millions of pinpricks of light illuminate the dark night, and almost in slow motion the bodyguard arches backwards, falls to the ground.

With the bodyguard dealt with I turn my attention back to Princess Anne, only to find that she has closed the door, and she and her husband, Captain Mark Phillips, are gripping the inside door handle and holding it firmly shut.

I grab the handle on my side and pull with all my might.

They pull with all their might.

The door isn't budging.

"Open or I'll shoot!" I yell, but they are strong, obdurate.

"What's going on here?" I turn to find a uniformed constable has appeared, is watching the struggle, trying to understand what is happening.

I'm not in the mood for conversation, so I point the gun and say tersely, "Go away or I'll shoot."

The copper peers past me at Princess Anne. "Come on sonny, don't be stupid."

I should have known that one of London's finest wouldn't be deterred by the mere sight of a gun, so I curl my finger around the trigger and squeeze. There is a dull whip-like crack and the constable doubles up in agony, topples over backwards.

Returning my attention to the Princess I see that her lady in waiting has escaped out of the other side of the car, but Anne and Captain Mark Phillips are still clutching the door handle with grim determination. I decide to try another approach. "Open up," I say, "this is important."

Anne glares at me. "Not bloody likely," she retorts.

Rumours of her bloody-minded nature are clearly not exaggerated.

"I need you to come with me," I tell her, but before I can explain further, there is another interruption.

"You bastard!" Before I can turn to see who is now wanting to play the hero, a vicious blow catches me on the back of the head. I stumble towards the car, then turn, my head still spinning, to find a young, well-built man, with a squashed boxer's nose, squaring up to have another go at me.

Still dazed, I do the only thing possible, pointing the gun at him and hollering, "Fuck off or I'll shoot!"

For a moment I think I'm going to have to shoot him too, but then he thinks better of it, backs away. How is one supposed to kidnap a Princess in The Mall on a damp March night with all these distractions, I wonder, as I look around me to see if there are any more bloody heroes.

The coast is clear so I turn back to the royal car only to discover that the chauffeur has climbed into the back of the car and is now also grabbing the door handle.

I point the .34 at the window. "Open the door or I'll fire!" I warn.

"I'm not getting out of the car," Princess Anne repeats.

Why is she so obstinate? Probably a lifetime of always getting what you want and doing what you please.

"Have it your way," I grumble as I fire at the window.

The safety glass shatters into milky opacity, and I have to clear the window using the butt of my gun to see inside, scattering small glass pebbles across the road and inside the car. When I peer inside I see that Princess Anne and the other two have exited through the kerbside door.

I sprint round the front of the car but when I reach the kerb I'm horrified to see two burly police officers bearing down on me at an alarming rate.

As I hesitate, Princess Anne sees my uncertainty. "Go on," she says. "Now's your chance to escape."

My plan is unravelling fast, but running away is not part of my agenda. As the officers close in on me I drop down on one knee, like a cowboy in a classic western, and take aim at the advancing coppers, but it is too late. As I raise my guns, they launch themselves at me, land on top of me, pinning me to the tarmac. The guns go flying from my hands and my head slams onto the hard ground with a loud crack.

I look up, half dazed, am greeted by a meaty fist pounding my face.

"Are you going to come quietly?" growls one of the coppers.

As the blood starts to flow from my nose I drift away. "Damn it! It wasn't supposed to go like this," is my last thought before I black out.

When I come to, I find myself pinned to the floor of a police car by the two oversized constables. Although I can't see anything, it is clear we are travelling at great speed, the tyres squealing with every corner, the engine revving hard, the siren wailing. I'm struggling to breathe beneath the weight of the coppers, my face squashed against the filthy floor, but just as I think I'm going to pass out again the car screeches to a halt and I am unceremoniously dragged out of the car, one copper gripping each arm, and into the bright lights of the police station.

Chapter 2

There are times when silence is worse than any words.

The police are purposeful, brutal, silent, no words needed as they throw me to the floor of the police station, begin punching and kicking me for the effrontery of attacking a member of the royal family. The only sound is their grunts of effort, my gasps of pain.

The Station Sergeant watches them dispassionately for a couple of minutes as they work me over, then finally calls them off. "That's enough," he says. "We need to get him processed before the press start sniffing around."

Reluctantly, gradually, like a rain storm running out of steam, they stop battering me, drag me to a holding cell which reeks of vomit and urine and sweat, strip me naked then throw me to the floor. The echo of the metal door slamming rings through my head as I look around. The cell is tiny, the sickening green walls covered with obscene anti-police graffiti. I wouldn't mind adding a few choice words to it after the pasting they've given me, but it would require too much effort. All I can do is crawl across the floor and onto a raised platform with a rock-hard mattress on it. I flop down on my back, gaze up at the dark sky through the tiny window high up in the wall.

I drift in and out of sleep, the events of the past few hours flashing in and out of my mind, a jumble of disordered events, my well-laid plan gradually descending into chaos, while Princess Anne looks on, shaking her head and repeating, "Not bloody likely," over and over again.

The rattling of keys drags me from my reverie. The door is flung open, rough hands grab me, and I am hauled out into the bright lights once more. The office is full. It seems like every copper within twenty miles has come to have a look at the man who tried to kidnap Princess Anne.

The Station Sergeant looks at me like something unpleasant that he has found on the sole of his shoe. "We're going to take your fingerprints," he tells me.

For some reason I'm feeling obdurate. "Piss off!" I tell him.

He gives a nod. Two coppers grab my legs, two grab my arms and shoulders, then hoist me into the air, hold me out flat like a sacrificial offering. About twenty coppers stare at me, stark naked, my somewhat inadequate manhood plain for all to see.

To my surprise, no ribald or insulting comments are forthcoming, and everyone manages to keep a straight face as the Sergeant takes prints from each of my fingers in turn, dabbing them on the ink pad and then on the paper. When he's finished, I am dragged back to my cell by a half dozen coppers.

"Thank you for your cooperation" says one, without a trace of irony in his voice.

"Bollocks!" I retort.

In response they slam the door so hard it nearly comes off its hinges.

I stagger back to the sanctuary of the mattress, curl up in the foetal position with my back to the door, close my eyes and try to sleep.

Once more I find sleep elusive, and am relieved when the door opens again and two uniformed constables toss me a set of clothes. "Get yourself dressed," one of them tells me, "you look disgusting naked."

I hold up the clothes – there's a natty pinstripe suit. I try it on and find to my surprise that it fits perfectly. As I finish buttoning the shirt I hear footsteps in the corridor outside, and a posse of four detectives swarm in.

They look around the cell with practised disdain before turning their attention to me. "I'm Deputy Assistant Commissioner Ernest Bond," says the oldest of them, sitting down on the mattress beside me. I can smell his aftershave, the great smell of Brut, see the patches of whiskers on his neck that he missed when he shaved this morning.

"Any relation to James?" I wonder.

Either he has no sense of humour, or he's heard it so many times that it doesn't even register with him any more.

"I'm in charge of your case," he continues. "I need you to answer a few questions for me."

I nod amiably. After the beatings I've taken from the police, answering a few questions is a welcome relief.

"What's your name?"

An easy one to start with. "You've taken my fingerprints and checked them," I reply, "so you should know already."

Bond keeps his poker face intact. "I would like you to confirm it."

"Ian Ball," I tell him.

"Where do you live?"

"17 Silverdale, Fleet, Hampshire"

"How old are you?"

"I was born on the 24th September 1947 and it's now the 20th March 1974. Work it out," I answer. Why should I do all the hard work?

"That makes you 26. Yes?"

I nod. He has a brain.

Bond glances at the other detectives, who are standing watching us, like wallflowers at a dance when the last available girl has just been swiped from under their noses, then returns his gaze to me.

"What were you doing in The Mall at 8.30 this evening?"

And so it begins…

"Well, I was driving along The Mall and I felt bored," I told him, "so I thought I would make life more interesting by attempting to kidnap Princess Anne and demanding a three-million-pound ransom."

The detectives glance amongst themselves.

"Were you alone?"

"No."

They all look shocked.

"Princess Anne was with me," I continue, "and various members of her entourage."

Bond sighs. "Were you alone in committing the attack?"

I nod. "Yes, completely. I'm a loner, I have no friends."

Bond looks at me, and just for an instant, I think I see sympathy in his eyes. "OK, that will do for now," he tells me. "I'll question you more fully later."

He stands and heads for the door, the other three scurrying out ahead of him. As he reaches the door he turns and looks back at me. "Do you want something to eat?"

Despite my surprise I manage a coherent reply. "Yes, a full English breakfast, please."

"I'll see what I can do."

I decide to press my luck. "And to go with it, a Vodka Martini, shaken not stirred."

A ghost of a smile crosses Bond's face. "Would you settle for a cup of tea?"

"If the cocktail waiter is busy, I guess it will have to do."

Bond softly closes the door behind him.

After half-an-hour, there is no sign of my meal, so I ask the policeman outside my cell door to find out what's happened to it. He disappears, returns shortly with the Station Sergeant in tow. The Station Sergeant is short, portly, stands with his hands on his hips and his belly thrust out as he talks. "I don't believe in feeding animals like you!" he tells me.

"But the detective said – "

The Sergeant cuts me off. "But the detective said," he mimics. He glares at me. "The detective doesn't run this station," he informs me. "You get fed when I say you get fed, and not a minute before." And with that, he turns on his heel and marches away.

So much for that.

There is nothing else to be done, so I carefully fold my jacket, set it at the head of the mattress as a pillow, and settle down to sleep. Amazingly, I soon drift off into a deep, dreamless sleep.

Chapter 3

"Wakey, wakey, rise and shine!" I am woken abruptly by a copper banging on my door with a night stick.

I jerk awake, momentarily confused by where I am. As I stare at the bilious green walls, the cold, concrete floor, it all comes back to me.

Two policemen enter the cell, and one of them gives me a tray on which is a full English breakfast and a mug of tea.

After a night in the cell I am famished, and quickly devour the sumptuous repast with enthusiasm, all the while watched by the two cops, who occupy their time by complaining about the canteen food. Their main complaint seems to be the greasy fried eggs, however, I don't find them to be greasy. When I have finished, I gulp down the tea, lean back in my bunk. "That was delicious, my compliments to the chef."

The coppers give me a look of disbelief. One of them takes the tray from me while the other grabs my arm and hauls me to my feet. "Come on."

"Where are we going?"

"Bow Street Magistrates Court."

He spins me around, clamps handcuffs on my wrists. The metal is cold against my skin. He hauls me towards the door.

"Don't I get to wash my face or clean my teeth first?" I protest.

The cop ignores me, drags me along a brightly lit corridor and down a long flight of stairs.

"My mother would be horrified if she knew, going out in public without washing first."

At the bottom of the stairs, a door opens out into a small

courtyard. A grey sky looms overhead, dank and oppressive, turning the cobblestones slick with rain as I am hustled into a waiting paddy wagon.

When we reach the van, the copper gives me a hand up.

"Thank you," I say reflexively.

"You're welcome," he replies.

Dashed polite these police officer chappies I think, as I settle into the back of the van, my handcuffs jingling.

I am driven to Bow Street Magistrates Court, where I am remanded into custody and sent to Brixton Prison. After three months in Brixton, I am tried at the Old Bailey, convicted of attempted kidnap and attempted murder and committed to Rampton Special Hospital.

The trial passes in a blur. The only part that remains clear in my mind is when I am given the opportunity to speak about what motivated my crime. I remember looking around the packed courthouse, all the serious faces, the judge glaring at me, my lawyer giving me nervous glances, wondering what I might say. "I would like to say that I did it because I wished to draw attention to the lack of facilities for treating mental illness under the National Health Service," I tell the court. Someone has to say it, right?

It's 3 o'clock on a sunny June afternoon when we arrive at Rampton. The journey is completed in record time as we had a police escort all the way. As I emerge from the van, I find that in contrast to the grim, grey, Victorian asylum I was expecting, the hospital buildings are modern red-brick structures with newly painted white windows. Maybe this won't be so bad I tell myself…

The screws lead me to my room. It is around five metres by three, with a small hatch in the door at head height, and a security lock which only a nurse can unlock. I peer into the room. There's a chamber pot on the right, an iron-framed bed to the right. I press on the mattress and the metal springs creak. The screw points to the end of the bed. "Bed pack," he tells me. The bed pack consists of folded sheets, blankets and a counterpane.

"You can't keep any personal possessions in your room," the screw continues, "everything has to be in your locker." He gives me a disconcerting smile that makes my skin crawl. "Make yourself at home, get your pyjamas on, and we'll get better acquainted later."

The screws depart and I change into the pyjamas they have provided, then lie on the bed, gaze up at the ceiling. There's a long strip light and a night light, and at the head of the bed is the outside wall, which has a large window in it, with a lockable shutter. The shutter is painted white, the walls a pale cream colour.

A well-dressed middle-aged man comes in, a clipboard in his hand. "I'm Doctor Foster," he informs me. "I'm here just to see if you have any immediate needs, then your case officer will see you tomorrow."

"I'm OK," I say amiably.

"No ailments, physical or mental?"

I shake my head.

"Are you on any medication?"

"No."

He ticks several boxes on his form, then looks up at me and smiles. "OK then." And with that he is gone.

I've barely settled back down on the bed when three nurses come in. I decide it is polite to get up and stand by the bed. They introduce themselves.

"I'm Charge Nurse Roach and this is Staff Nurse Flame and S.E.N. Dante."

Roach is of average height, with swept back greying hair and a tight, pinched face. He gives a wicked smile, holds up a razor and a can of shaving foam. "We've come to shave your beard off," he informs me.

I frown. "Why do I have to have my beard shaved, it's just a small goatee, not a big bushy beard."

Again Roach gives his wicked smile. "It's the rules," he

informs me, "and you do want to follow the rules, don't you?"

"Of course," I reply, "but in prison it's up to the governor whether or not someone has to have their beard shaved off. Can I see the superintendent?"

"We haven't got a superintendent." Roach says it almost gleefully, "We set the rules."

"A doctor then?"

Roach's patience is wearing thin. "Never mind the fucking doctors, we run this place!" he shouts, indicating his fellow nurses.

"I'm not having it shaved until I see a doctor," I assert.

Roach gives another crocodile smile. "Gentlemen, we have a trouble maker," he says as the three advance on me. Roach's hands go for my throat, his sweaty palms wrapping themselves around my neck while his fingers press into my spine, crushing my windpipe and cutting off my air supply. He's done this before.

As I start to gasp he slams my head against the wall, brings his face close to mine, eyes blazing, spittle flying. "Listen to me, you pathetic little bastard. I've dealt with your sort a thousand times. Either you have your beard shaved, or we'll cut off your balls and feed them to the dogs!"

I gasp, my eyes watering. His halitosis is atrocious.

Without warning he hammers his right knee up into my groin. As I double forward in agony the other two join in, raining blows down on my head and body until I crumple to the floor.

His grin still firmly in place, Roach falls on my chest with one knee, sinking deep into my diaphragm. Dizziness threatens to overwhelm me, shock, pain and surprise mixing together. Before I can catch my breath he grabs my balls and squeezes hard. The pain is excruciating but I refuse to cry out.

As Roach stands up, Flame and Dante wade in, kicking me with all their might. Luckily the force of their kicks propels me under the bed where they can't get at me. I force myself back against the wall, hands held protectively in front of me in preparation of the next assault, listen to the trio cursing and swearing as they discuss what to do. Footsteps approach, other people enter the room. We're attracting quite a crowd.

I am too stunned to think clearly, desperately try to catch my breath, hoping against hope that they will decide this is too much trouble, leave me alone to lick my wounds.

My hopes are immediately dashed as Roach kneels down, peers at me as I cower under the bed. "Little pig, little pig, let me come in," he chants, then thrusts out a hand, grabs my hair and hauls me out from beneath the bed. I look up at seven nurses, all bound and determined to see me submit to Roach, to the rules, to the system.

The other six grab me, dump me on the bed, pin me in place.

Roach leans over me, strokes my beard. "What do we think, gentlemen? Shaving cream or no shaving cream?" He waggles a can of shaving cream in the air.

"I think he's lost his right to niceties like shaving cream," says Flame.

"We shouldn't waste it on a trouble maker like this," agrees Dante.

"Very well." Roach tosses the can away over his shoulder. I hear it hit the wall, roll across the floor. "No shaving foam it is."

Roach presses the razor against my cheek, scrapes it down my face. The pain is immense as each vicious stroke rips my skin to shreds, each one designed to inflict the maximum amount of pain rather than actually remove much hair.

As Roach scrapes away my beard and my skin he studies my face intensely, looking for any signs of distress.

I show none.

Remain relaxed and calm, I tell myself, imagine he's giving me a relaxing facial massage.

Finally, Roach finishes, stands up and admires his handiwork. "Very nice," he grins. The others troop out, until only Roach remains. He leans over me, grabs my bloody chin. "Oh dear, Mister Ball," he says. "You appear to have cut yourself shaving." His venomous eyes bore into mine. "And if you tell anyone anything different, well, let's just say this will seem like a pleasant evening between friends compared to what you'll get next time."

I lie very still, feel the blood trickling down my face, too traumatised to do anything more than lie staring up at the ceiling.

Welcome to Rampton.

Chapter 4

"Get up Ball!"

Still half asleep, I jump out of bed as two screws walk in. These are new guys, different from the ones who beat me last night, but I decide that for right now I'll assume they are all violent psychopaths.

"Take your mattress off so that we can check the springs."

I take the mattress off, watch as one of them examines my springs while the other unlocks the shutter. Without another word they walk out.

"Good morning Ian. How are you today? Did you sleep well?" I mutter to myself. "It's a beautiful day today," I add. I might as well say it to myself, clearly no one else is going to say it.

I'm still none the wiser about the schedule, I assume I am supposed to make the bed, so that is what I do, then step outside and put on my socks and slippers, which are on the floor outside my door.

I look around. Everybody seems to be going to the office, so I follow them, find they are all collecting their locker keys. I get mine, get my towel and soap from my locker, head for the washroom.

I am obviously not moving fast enough, as a screw bellows, "hurry up Ball," as I shuffle down the corridor. I increase my speed by a barely perceptible amount, reach the washroom, find a place at a vacant sink.

I peer at my face in the mirror. It's a mess of scabs and blood trails. I clean myself up as best I can, brush my teeth, get dressed.

As I am leaving, a screw snarls, "where's your tie?"

I've only been awake ten minutes and already I've had enough of being shouted at.

"It's in my pocket," I reply.

The screw glares at me.

"What's it doing there?"

I pull open my pocket and peer in. "It's not doing anything," I say, "it's just sort of lying there."

The screw moves closer, eyeball to eyeball.

"Don't be a cheeky bastard," he hisses, "just put it on."

I head back into the bathroom, put on my tie with the aid of a mirror.

The screw is waiting for me when I reappear. I waggle my tie at him. "Happy?"

"Put your towel away and come back and get a bucket," he shouts.

He's obviously not happy.

I look down the end of the corridor, see the cleaning equipment being handed out. I get my bucket, scrubbing brush, cloth and a rubber kneeling pad, return to where the screw stands. "Where do I start?"

"Where do I start, what?" he growls.

I am mystified.

"Where do I start, sir," he explains. "You call me sir."

I frown. "Are you sure?"

"Yes I'm bleeding sure!" he roars.

Very well. I stand to attention, click my heels together and raise my head until I'm staring at the ceiling. "Where do I go, sir!" I shout.

The screw looks livid, like he is going to launch an attack at any moment, but manages to control himself. "There. Down the end!"

"Yes, sir, thank you, sir, very kind of you, sir!" I reply as I saunter down to the end of the corridor. I kneel down, start scrubbing.

The screw follows me, watches what I'm doing. "Don't scrub the redwork," he tells me.

There is a thin strip of red concrete on either side of the floor. I wipe the soap off the redwork, begin scrubbing the lino between the redwork. After a couple of minutes I've finished this bit, so I look round to see if I can move down. There is a line of patients along the corridor, all of whom seem to be scrubbing the same bit of lino over and over again. Oh well, when in Rome, I decide, continue listlessly scrubbing the same few square inches of floor.

A pair of black, shiny shoes appear in my line of sight, I look up, see Doctor Foster looking down at me with concern. He winces when he sees my scab covered face.

"Sorry about what happened to you yesterday."

I shrug. "That's OK, it's not your fault."

"Best to keep your head down," he says, then shakes my hand, winks, and hurries away.

I'm scrubbing my bit of lino for about the tenth time when the screw shouts, "Breakfast!"

We all stop working, put our stuff away and line up outside the dining room. I lean against the wall with my hands in my pockets in my normal relaxed manner.

The screw marches up to me. "The wall doesn't need propping up, Ball!"

I slowly resume an upright position.

"And take your hands out of your pockets. If you want to play with your pathetic pecker, do it in the privacy of your own room."

I slowly take my hands out of my pockets, shake and move them around, looking from one to the other as though I don't know what to do with them.

The screw goes to the dining room, peers inside, announces, "Breakfast's ready," and we all file in.

I sit at a table, stare at the plate I've been given. There's a thin, pale sausage, an egg, and a cup of a mud-coloured liquid. I stab the sausage and dip it into the egg, bite off a mouthful, chew and swallow. Two bites and it's gone. Two more mouthfuls and the egg is gone too. That's it, four mouthfuls. Quality excellent, quantity miserly.

I take a sip of the liquid and grimace. I had assumed it was tea, but I'm having second thoughts. "God, what's this?"

The screw marches over. "Shut up Ball, you're not allowed to talk at the dining table!"

Perhaps sugar will improve it? I look around, don't see any on the table. I contemplate asking the screw, but he is still glaring at me, an angry look on his face. Perhaps another day.

When everyone has finished the cutlery is counted and we are discharged.

As I head towards the door, my name rings out once more. "Ball! Put your chair under the table!"

I grab hold of the back of the chair and manoeuvre it under the table. That would be enough to satisfy the screw, but if they want to play games, I can do the same.

I crouch down, move the chair a millimetre, observing it closely, then straighten up, make another minor adjustment, stand back and admire my handiwork. Nope, not quite right. A slight shake of my head before I bend down again and make another microscopic adjustment, before once more stepping back and admiring my handiwork. With a small nod, I calmly walk out past the red-faced screw.

I catch up with the herd in the day room, settle down on the couch next to another inmate. He picks his nose, looks at me with interest. "You're the new guy."

"That's me, the new guy." I hold out my hand. "I'm Ian, what's your name?"

"Ozzy."

"Hi Ozzy. So what do we do now?"

"We wait here until our names are called then go to the office for our medication."

"And when everybody's taken their medication?"

Ozzy picks his nose again, examines the contents. "Work. You'll either be scrubbing the floor or using a decker."

I give him a quizzical look.

"A decker is a large, heavy, rectangular brush on the end of a long pole," he explains. "You move it backwards and forwards to shine the floor."

"That sounds like interesting and challenging work."

Ozzy studies my face. He is apparently immune to sarcasm. His eyes roam over my lacerated, scabby face and neck. "They did you over proper good last night."

I nod. "Bunch of psychos."

"This shift isn't too bad, but Roach's shift are all psychopaths," Ozzy informs me. He licks his lips nervously, looks around to be sure no one is listening to him. "Flame mostly slaps, Dante punches, but Roach, he's the one, he has the reputation as the most brutal screw in the hospital."

"I had the pleasure of their company last night," I inform him.

He glances at my face once more. "I've seen worse."

I don't know whether to be comforted or horrified.

"Work up!" the screw shouts.

"Have fun," Ozzy tells me as he climbs to his feet. Maybe he does have a sense of humour…

"Ball!"

I've been mopping the floor for nearly an hour. The screw marches up to me. "The RMO wants to see you." He heads off down the corridor, with me in tow, directs me to the interview room, knocks on the door.

"Come!"

The screw opens the door, shoves me inside. "Behave yourself, you hear me?"

The interview room is small, two chairs separated by a table, a screw standing watch in one corner. A non-descript man sits at the table, looks up as I come in.

"I'm doctor Hazzard. I'm your RMO. RMO stands for Responsible Medical Officer. I'm the doctor responsible for your care." He motions for me to sit. "What mental problems do you have?" he asks breezily.

"None whatsoever."

Hazzard scowls, scans his notes.

While he reads I take the chance to study him. He's small-framed, with thinning hair, and despite the fact that he's wearing a suit and tie, he somehow manages to look scruffy. I'd guess he's mid to late thirties, though he looks older.

"You told Dr Scott in Brixton that you were hearing voices, that you were depressed, that you felt persecuted?" The question is thrown out as a challenge.

I cross my legs, stare back at him. "I made all that up because I wanted to go to a hospital instead of a prison."

Another scowl. "I see. So you've never been ill?"

"Before the incident involving Princess Anne I was depressed," I admit.

"So you're a depressive?"

"Dr Scott said I was depressed because I had become completely isolated. He said it is quite normal to get depressed when you're isolated."

My reply seems to flummox Hazzard. "So you don't need me to prescribe any medication?"

"No, thank you."

Hazzard forces a fake smile to his face. "How are you getting on here?"

I point to my face. "I was beaten up by the screws last night, then they shaved me without any shaving foam."

He peers at my face. "The staff did this? And they beat you up?" He glances warily at the screw stationed in the corner of the room. "Who exactly?"

"Mr Roach, Mr Flame and Mr Dante exactly."

"Why did they beat you up?"

"Because I wanted to see a doctor before having my beard shaved off."

"That all sounds most irregular," he concludes. "I'll make enquiries." With that unpleasantness out of the way, he forces his smile back into place. "Is there anything else I can do for you?"

I shake my head. "No. Thanks."

And with that my first interview with Dr. Hazzard comes to a close.

I'm hoping that lunch will make up for the paucity of breakfast, but as I stare at the spoonful of mince on my plate I can see a pattern developing. I wolf it down, hoping that maybe dessert will be better, but all we get is a small pot of yoghurt. After scraping the pot clean I'm still famished. Clearly the bastards are trying to starve us into submission.

After lunch and medication (apparently, Hazzard has put me on Nardil antidepressant tablets), it's back to work. As I scrub, a nervous, smiling face appears in front of me.

"Hello Ian, I'm the vicar".

I was wondering what that white strip around your neck was, I think.

"You're down as C of E," he tells me.

"I used to be C of E," I tell him, "now I'm an atheist"

He covers his disappointment well. "Why don't you come to church on Sunday. It will get you off the ward for a while."

"No thanks."

"What's your singing voice like? Would you consider joining the choir?" I have to admire his persistence, but singing is not for me. I decline.

He studies me thoughtfully. It's disconcerting, as his left eyeball keeps on sinking to the bottom of the eye socket, then popping back up again. It looks like the sun setting over the horizon on a summer's evening, then suddenly returning like a shopper who forgot to get the milk.

"We have a bridge club," he says cheerily. "Do you play bridge?"

Again I decline.

Finally, reluctantly, he moves on, zeroing in another hapless sinner.

"Pack up!" Another shouted order, and once more I follow the herd as we all pack up, put on our outside shoes, then file, two abreast, like little kiddies on a school outing, to the exercise yard.

It's a barren gravel courtyard, with just a glimpse of blue sky above between the buildings. I walk around in circles, grateful of the chance to get some fresh air, but most of the other inmates seem beyond caring whether they are inside or out. They either sit on benches, or stand around talking and smoking.

The rest of the day is a haze of tightly scheduled leisure. Back inside at 3.30 to gaze at the TV, dinner at 5:00 (a hot dog and a mousse), then return to the dayroom until it's time for meds and then bed.

Chapter 5

While it might sound benign, boring even, it's as well to remember that Rampton is a psychiatric hospital, and one of the last places you ever want to wind up. My time there has seared it forever on my brain. Even now, when my mind drifts back there, I can picture it down to the last detail.

The 'L' shaped ward is accessed through a locked door which opens onto the main corridor. A few yards along the corridor, on the right, is the kitchen. The scullery man is the only patient allowed in the kitchen.

Next to the kitchen is the dining room. As soon as you go in there is a serving hatch on the right, and opposite this is a door that leads into the day room. The far wall of the dining room is taken up by windows. There are eight tables, each with four chairs, and on each table are the usual condiments.

Opposite the dining room is the ward office, and on the wall by the door is a wooden board with thirty hooks on it for the patients to hang their locker keys. There are thirteen side rooms running up the left-hand side of the main corridor.

Early morning. I wander into the day room. Two nurses are sitting chatting, they barely look up as I come in, though I know they are watching me. It's human nature, everyone wants to see how the new boy behaves, especially after my performance on admission. Will I continue to be trouble, or will I settle down and behave myself? I don't want trouble, so I wander quietly around the room taking in the lie of the land.

At the far end of the room is a door that leads into the dining room, and to the left of the door, running along the entire length of the back wall, are the patients' lockers, in which the patients keep their food, toiletries, stationery, etc. You can keep your locker key on you during the day, but must hand them into the office at night.

One wall has a 22 inch colour TV, securely located on a high shelf, and if the patients want to write letters or play games there are two tables at the back of the room near the lockers.

Wandering down the main corridor I pass the utility room, where a patient hands out overalls, buckets, scrubbing brushes, and deckers at work time, and further down, on the short corridor, is the clothes store, where the patients exchange their pyjamas for their day clothes every morning, then switch them back again each night.

Further on from the clothes store are the washrooms, and finally, at the far end of the corridor, the dormitory. This is carpeted, with nine beds and a toilet. It is considered a privilege to be a dormitory patient, and patients who sleep there are allowed to use their radios with headphones, unlike the patients in the side rooms.

As I return to the day room I hear a voice close behind me. "What's your name?"

I turn to see a thin, almost cadaverous man looking at me.

Before I can reply he thrusts his hand out towards me. "I'm Timothy, but everyone calls me 'Rail', because, you know, I'm thin as a rail."

"Hi. I'm Ian."

He glances over at the screws. "They hate us, you know."

I follow his gaze. The two screws are looking at us with interest. I pretend to look away, then study them while pretending to look at Timothy.

"The older one is Roach," he tells me. "That's his real name. Like most of them, he lives to inflict pain. If he's in a bad mood, which is almost every day, he doesn't wait for you to do something wrong, he just starts shouting and hitting."

"We've met. He's a real charmer." I give a bitter laugh.

Timothy's face turns serious. "Don't laugh. If they see you

laughing they assume you're up to something."

"And what about the other? He was also part of my welcome party."

Roach's companion has thick lips and a large bulbous nose, stares at us with beady eyes.

"That's Flame. He's not as outright violent as Roach, but he loves to inflict punishment."

"Punishment? Are they allowed to punish us?" I had assumed that my beating was an introductory special, not something that might occur on a regular basis.

Timothy leads me away to the far side of the room, where we drop into two battered green armchairs. "This whole place is built around punishments," he tells me. "It's the glue that holds Rampton together."

A queasy feeling settles itself deep in my stomach. I had assumed that being in a psych hospital would be better, more liberal, than being in prison.

"Punishments are graded according to severity," Timothy tells me. He gives a nervous glance around, his small, furtive eyes reminding me of a mouse caught out in the open, licks his dry lips. "It starts with Level One."

"What's Level One?"

"Extra work detail."

"That doesn't sound so bad. At least you won't be bored."

"You might think that. But it's brutal – they make you spend the whole day on your knees scrubbing the floor, then send you to bed early."

"I'm sure I could manage that for a day or two," I reply, trying to sound unperturbed.

"A day or two?" Timothy gives a dry cackle that makes his Adam's Apple bounce. "Try telling that to Wilson." He nods towards an older man with thin silver hair, who is listlessly scrubbing a small patch of floor in the corner. I realise he's been there ever since I arrived. "He's been on Level One work detail since Easter."

I do a quick calculation. It's over two months. "What did he do wrong?"

"Called Flame a child molester."

I glance over at Flame. It's probably a fair assessment, but I make a mental note not to ever mention it.

Timothy fidgets in his seat, crossing and uncrossing his legs. "Level Two is an increase to your medication, which as everything they give you has severe and debilitating side effects means you feel like shit the entire time."

I resist the urge to make a glib reply this time. This is serious and disconcerting.

Timothy leans in closer. "Level Three is isolation." His voice drops to a whisper.

"They strip you naked, then sling you into a cell with just a mattress and a piss pot. For the first couple of days you get nothing to eat, and then, if the screws are feeling humorous, they might give you a tiny pea in the centre of a large dinner plate." He shudders. "I was in there for two weeks once, with a big dose of Level Four mixed in."

"Level Four?"

"Good old fashioned physical brutality. Beating, kicking, slapping, anything that inflicts pain."

The queasy feeling is growing stronger, and my mind is starting to wonder what I can do to avoid – or indeed incur – these punishments.

"Then there's Level Five," Timothy continues, almost gleefully. "ECT."

I have the vague feeling I've heard of ECT, but can't quite put my finger on it.

"Electroconvulsive therapy," Timothy explains. "They hook you up to this machine that sends electric shocks through your brain." He leans in even closer, grabs my arm tight. "It results in irreversible brain damage and permanent memory loss."

My brain is reeling. I feel like I've been admitted to Dante's nine circles of Hell, each one more horrific than the last. I hardly dare to ask what Level Six might be.

Timothy glances over at the screws, then grins as he tells me.

"Level Six? That's the worst of all. You have to see your RMO, who talks you to death for what feels like years."

He looks up, sees Flame waddling towards us. He has a peculiar walk, with his butt thrust out and swaying from side to side. He stops in front of us, puts his hands on his hips. "What are you two girls gossiping about?" he shouts.

Timothy looks down at his feet. "Nothing, sir. I was just introducing the new guy to the ward."

Flame glares at him for a moment, then shouts, "Well don't!"

He turns his attention to me. "New bloke. On your feet."

I stand quickly, almost bumping into Flame, he is standing so close to us.

He takes a step back. "Assessment Centre for you." He nods towards the corridor. -"That way, quick march."

I double-time it across the room, Flame waddling behind me. At the end of the corridor he opens a door, shoves me inside. "New one for you," he says, "see if he's as useless as he looks."

The assessment centre is a welcome relief from the tense, hostile atmosphere in the main ward. The tasks are menial – painting plaster gnomes, making fishing nets or baskets, weaving stool seats, making wooden handles for bags, but the staff here don't shout, don't hit, don't belittle or insult the patients.

Three screws watch over ten male and five female patients, and I come to look forward to the four hours each day that I spend there. I keep myself busy, and use the opportunity to observe the other patients.

There are thirty patients on the ward, aged between 21 – 60, with IQs ranging from 70 to 140. Their crimes are equally diverse, everything from murder to shoplifting, and I have to confess that I soon learned to avoid most of them.

In contrast to the relaxed atmosphere of the Assessment Centre, the ward is always tense and oppressive. The patients hate the screws and the screws hate the patients, treating them as worthless sub-human creatures. They never address a patient in a normal tone of voice, always shout. They never praise, always criticise and condemn. Insults are the lingua franca of the ward, with their favourite targets being the intelligence of the patients, their personal hygiene, and of course their parentage. And when insults aren't enough? Well there's always physical abuse as a trusted stand by.

Chapter 6

Another day, another gentle awakening.

"Get up, Ball, you moronic bastard!"

I awake with a start, but before I can get my wits about me, Flame and Dante are all over me. They each grab a corner of the mattress and tip me out onto the floor. I hit the floor with a thud, roll over and sit up. Before I have the chance to even get to my feet, they have checked my springs, unlocked the shutter, and are making their way out of the room. As he goes, Flame shouts, "Hurry up, dickhead!"

As I peel off my pyjamas I check my body for bruises. I have a couple of beauties from the welcoming party the first night, but the soreness is starting to recede.

My first job of the day is to make the bed. I already have a routine for doing so.

Firstly, I place the pillows at the head of the bed, then go to the foot and make the bed pack. Next, I fold the blankets into a rectangle and place them on top of each other, then fold the two sheets and place them on top of the blankets. Lastly, I fold the counterpane so that it is exactly the width of the bed pack and wrap it round. When I'm finished, I stand back and admire my handiwork – beautiful, a work of art.

For breakfast we have a tiny rolled-up bit of bacon. At least I think it's bacon. It's so small that when you put it in your mouth and swallow, it's gone before you have the chance to taste it. Maybe that's just as well.

Work duty. I present myself at the utility room where Flame and Dante are giving out the buckets and deckers. Dante gives me a decker. Flame panics, shouts, "no!" as he takes the decker from me.

Dante gives him a quizzical look.

"He's too stupid to use a decker," explains Flame as he shoves a bucket into my hands.

I pick a spot half way along the corridor and start to scrub. After scrubbing the same bit for 4 or 5 minutes, I see Flame approaching with his curious, waddling gait. As he passes he aims a vicious kick at my bucket. The bucket goes flying in the air, spilling water all over the floor.

Flame looks down at me, his thick lips quivering. "Oops, how clumsy of me," he says. "You'd better clean it up."

Resisting my natural urge to say, "Get stuffed Flame", I instead reply, "Yes sir." It's too early in the day to endure another beating, but I still want to have some fun, so I pick up my cloth, carefully fold it, then throw it at a puddle of water near Flame's shoes. Flame has to take a hurried step to the side to avoid being splashed.

"Oops," I say, "how clumsy of me."

Flame glares at me, and I tense up waiting for the inevitable kick in my direction, but at that moment Dr Hazzard breezes down the corridor towards us, tie askew, white coat flapping, smiling nervously at everyone. "Good morning," he chirps as he passes. "Are we all doing well today?"

Flame gives me a last hateful look then retreats to the end of the corridor, watches Hazzard until he disappears into his office.

As soon as the coast is clear, Flame marches back towards me, his path directly in line with my bucket. I wait until he is just a few feet away, then in an exaggerated movement, I drop down on my bucket, put my arms around and hug it with all my might.

Flame is confused by my actions. He stops, stares at me. "You're a few bricks short of a load, Ball," he growls. "Dick head!" And with that he marches off and leaves me in peace.

I wait until he is a couple of yards away, then turn round and give a massive 'V' sign to his back, much to the amusement of the other patients.

After our tea break I am back in the same spot, but I have learnt from my encounter with Flame – instead of having a full bucket, I have only half a bucket of water. This way, if it gets kicked over again, I'll have only half as much to mop up.

As I scrub at my patch of floor I see Flame creeping up on Rail, who is obviously not decking as fast as Flame would like. As Flame reaches him, Rail turns around, just in time for Flame to deliver a vicious slap to the side of Rail's head. Rail staggers backwards, shocked and dazed, and Flame walks away with a strange gait. I'm sure that he's got an erection from the sexual thrill of hitting a patient.

Shaving time, and to my dismay, Flame is in charge of shaving today. I take an electric shaver, work my way around the scabs and shave as best I can.

"Hurry up, Ball, you cretin!" shouts Flame.

I ignore him, keep shaving.

He moves closer to me, almost in my pocket. "How can this take so long?" he hisses. "You're just plain stupid, aren't you? As much use as an inflatable dart board."

I try to focus on my shaving, but it's hard to concentrate with Flame breathing down my neck.

He moves even closer. "Ball, you're an imbecile aren't you?"

He holds out his hand. "If you don't give me that shaver right now I will ram it down your throat!"

I point to a spot on my face, "Can I just."

"No you can't."

"But I just…"

"Last warning." He cracks his knuckles ominously.

"Christ!" I slam the shaver down into Flame's hand and storm out. As I walk down the corridor I hear a whole litany of swear words, some of which are new even to me, but thankfully Flame doesn't chase me down.

After another minuscule lunch, Dante marches up to me, and I finally hear some words that brighten my day. "It's canteen day today," he announces, "so make out a list of goodies you want from the shop and give it to me. You'll get them after tea".

I scan the list of provisions, looking for something, anything, that I can eat. My eyes fall on the blessed words Ritz Crackers. I order five boxes, figuring that they are cheap and filling and should help with the hunger pains caused by the hospital's starvation diet.

There is another hour of scrubbing and decking to endure before we are allowed outside into the exercise yard. I settle down to scrubbing the same bit of floor that I have already scrubbed twenty times this morning, the screws' constant curses, insults and threats assaulting my ears. After a short while Dante creeps past me, his thin, athletic frame tense with excitement and anticipation. Dante is younger than most of the screws, maybe twenty-five, and looks like a decent, upstanding bloke, but beneath the ready smile and the clever one-liners lies the heart of a psychopath. Dante loves abusing inmates, and the more creative the method the better.

As I watch, Dante tiptoes towards the fire doors that partition the corridor. Right now the doors are open, and a patient can be half seen, kneeling on the floor between the open door and the wall, daydreaming, not working.

Dante smiles as he nears his target, unseen, like a cat closing in on an unsuspecting mouse. When he reaches the door Dante pauses for just a second, savouring the moment, then kicks it with all his might. The door slams against the patient, crushing him up against the wall. He cries out in pain and surprise, then collapses to the floor, blood already pouring from his nose, dripping onto the floor.

Dante looks down on him, smiling. "Oy! Numb skull? Clean up that bloody mess!" He seems very pleased with his joke. "Clean up that bloody mess!" He turns to me. "Bloody mess? Get it?"

When I don't laugh he shakes his head, marches off, grinning to himself.

The exercise yard is a blessed relief from the ward. The sun is shining, so I sit on a bench and read a magazine, grateful for some sun and fresh air on my skin.

A patient comes up and stands a couple of feet away, peers at me from under shaggy eyebrows. He's in his forties, thin and angular, with long arms and legs.

He continues to stare at me, but I avoid eye contact. I've already learned that it's best to avoid engaging with most of the other patients, they are either too deranged to make any sense, or too dangerous to want to be around.

The next thing I know the patient has slammed a fist into my eye. I topple backwards off the bench, look for my attacker.

"Get away Coogan!" the screw shouts.

Coogan has stationed himself over me, fists clenched, clearly ready to attack me again. "He violated my Princess Anne," he wails.

Dante trots over, grabs Coogan by the shoulder and shoves him away. Muttering, he retreats to the other side of the yard.

Dante grins at me as I climb to my feet, gingerly touch my eye. It's very tender.

"Coogan's madly in love with Princess Anne," explains Dante, "has pictures of her plastered all over his cell walls. Word's got around about what you did, it was only a matter of time before he came looking for you."

I peer over Dante's shoulder to where Coogan stands watching us. "What if the bastard does it again?"

"He won't." Dante sets off towards Coogan. "Follow me." He marches up to Coogan, who is still glaring at me. "This is Ball," Dante tells him. "He didn't hurt Princess Anne, he just wanted to talk to her."

Coogan seems unconvinced.

Dante tries another approach. "If you hit him again I'll take all your pictures of Princess Anne down, shit on them, then burn them. Understand?"

This gets Coogan's attention. He redirects his gaze from me to Dante. "Shit on my pictures?"

"Then burn them."

Coogan considers this for a moment, then says, "OK, I won't hit him again."

Dante seems pleased with his diplomacy skills. "There you go, all sorted."

After another measly dinner, our canteen supplies are given out. I immediately devour two boxes of Ritz Crackers and wash them down with a bottle of Coke. For the first time since arriving here I feel full. Life here isn't all bad, I say to myself, as I settle into bed that night…

Chapter 7

I soon realise that life in Rampton is a war of attrition. There are the screws and there are the inmates, and it is abundantly clear that most of the screws see it as their sacred mission to make life as difficult as possible for the inmates, whether that is through over-rigid enforcement of the rules, copious and creative insults, or sheer brutality.

I have quickly settled into a routine that includes keeping a diary and working on my autobiography, both of which I do in the evening, during TV time.

When bedtime is called, I collect my toothbrush and toothpaste and head to the washroom. It's locked.

Flame is lurking nearby, so polite as you please I ask, "Excuse me Mr Flame, could you unlock the washroom?"

Flame looks at me with undisguised disgust. "No!" he barks. "The washroom is never opened at this time."

I'm puzzled. It is, after all, bedtime. "I want to clean my teeth," I protest.

He simply glares at me, shouts "No!"

I try reason. "I clean my teeth before going to bed every night."

"Well, you can't tonight!"

So much for reason. "I'll go and see the Charge," I inform him.

To my surprise, the Charge overrules Flame. This enrages Flame, but he has no choice. The washroom is unlocked and I get to clean my teeth.

Flame, of course, stands by the washroom door muttering insults and curses the whole time I am cleaning my teeth.

When I finally finish, I pass Flame in the corridor on my way to my room, make sure to offer an exaggerated, "Thank you, sir," as I pass.

This enrages Flame even more.

Why the exaggerated politeness?

Firstly, it's self-preservation. As noted, the screws are brutes who will seize upon any excuse to abuse the inmates. It didn't take me long to realise that Roach, Dante, and especially Flame, who seems to have quickly formed a deep and personal antipathy towards me, need to be handled carefully.

Secondly, however, and perhaps more crucially, was the fact that I was not intending to be there for long, indeed should not be there for long. As you will discover, I had compelling reasons to believe that my release was imminent. But in the meantime it was paramount that I survive with my skin, and my sanity intact. And that meant playing along with their petty games, and ensuring that matters never got out of hand. Thus, while the screws were frequently loud, aggressive and abusive, I made it a point to always keep my cool, be polite, say yes sir and no sir, all the while going about my business.

One tactic which did seem to rile them was threatening to get a public enquiry into Rampton to uncover their abuse and violent treatment of the inmates. Mention of his was guaranteed to invoke the wrath of Flame and Dante, but interestingly, whenever I mentioned it to Roach, he simply smiled and informed me that it would never happen. I wondered what inspired such confidence on Roach's part, especially as I had assiduously recorded key incidents of the abuse, not just to myself, but also to other inmates, detailing chapter and verse of date, time, and actions. I was confident that I would soon have sufficient evidence to sink the whole sorry lot of them. However, I had counted without Roach's cunning.

After breakfast and work detail we have some spare time, so I head for my locker to retrieve my diary and update my notes. All patients have a locker where they can keep personal items, with the keys kept in the office. Thus only the inmate themselves, or the screws, can ever have access to your locker.

As I reach my locker, I spot Roach on the other side of the room, smiling at me. "Morning, Ball," he chirps as I unlock my locker and look inside. He's in an unusually happy mood, I think.

And then I realise – it's gone! My precious diary. Well, not gone exactly, but rather, ransacked, edited, redacted. I have been keeping my observations on a notepad, and while the notepad is still there, all the pages relating to my stay at Rampton have been ripped out, leaving just a few pages containing notes about my time before I was sent to Rampton.

Frustrated and furious, I look over at Roach. He is still grinning at me. "Everything OK, Ball?" he calls out. "You look a little worked up."

"My diary's been stolen!" I howl in protest.

Roach gives an obviously fake frown, like an actor in a 1920s silent film. "Stolen?" he gasps. "That's highly unlikely, wouldn't you say? Only you and the staff have access to the keys."

I look impotently back and forth between Roach and the vandalised diary.

Roach struts over to where I stand, points at the remains of my diary. "What's that then?"

"That's my notebook," I explain, "but most of the pages have been taken. There, you can see where they have been ripped out."

He peers at the offending pages like Sherlock Holmes investigating a particularly baffling mystery. "Yes, yes, I can see that," he says. "But the funny thing is, Ball, I distinctly remember seeing you tearing pages out of your notepad and eating them yesterday. I noted it in the shift notes if you'd like to see? What was it I wrote? Ball seems to have developed a taste for literature." He grins at his own joke.

"That's an outright lie!"

Again the fake frown. "That's quite a serious accusation, Ball. Delusional, accusative, those are negative traits that I'm sure Doctor Hazzard will want to discuss with you when next you meet. He'll probably have to increase your medication…" He gives a cheery smile and struts away. "Have a lovely day, Ball."

As I watch his retreating back it begins to dawn on me just how much of a challenge this is going to be. It's game on.

My mind was still churning over the events of the morning as I line up for the Assessment Centre. I quite enjoy the Assessment Centre, we get to work on a variety of arts and crafts type projects, with the hope that we will show an aptitude for one of them, which will then become our work assignment.

As we stand outside the door waiting to be admitted, there is some cheering from the front of the line, and the patients begin to crowd around an open doorway. Overcome by natural curiosity, I join the crowd to see what is happening. The corridor is part of a female ward, and a female patient is having a bath at that time. When she finishes, she emerges from the bathroom naked, much to the delight of the male patients.

"That's not right," I mutter, averting my eyes. The woman is clearly not fully compos mentis, has no idea of the show she is putting on.

"Looks all right to me," says another patient, ogling the woman. "Best part of the day it is, seeing her with her kit off."

I scowl. "You mean this happens every day?"

He grins. "You bet."

When we get back to the ward, I explain what I have seen to the Charge, pointing out that while the patient may be seriously disturbed, she is still entitled to be treated with the same dignity and respect as any other woman. To my surprise, when we line up for the Assessment Centre the following morning, a portable screen has been put up in the corridor to shield the female patient from the male patients' gaze and protect her modesty. There are howls of protest from the male patients, but I am pleased to see that on this occasion, at least, someone's dignity and rights have been respected.

Chapter 8

"Ball?" I am sitting quietly reading a magazine when Roach's voice summons me.

I look up.

"Case Conference, dining room, now," he orders.

Typical Roach, not a please or a thank you or a by your leave, but I nonetheless smile politely, get up and follow him into the dining room.

A case conference is a serious event, where the RMO (in my case Hazzard), nurses, and other professionals involved in the patient's case come together to discuss the situation and decide which ward they should send the patient to.

I enter the dining room, find Hazzard sitting at a table, flanked by two unknown men. Roach directs me to a chair facing the table, seats himself to my right. There's another unknown male to my left.

Hazzard is his usual scruffy self. How does the man make a jacket and tie look untidy? Hazzard coughs, gives his weak smile, wades right in. "You know why we're here," he begins, "so how are you mentally and physically"

"Both my mental and physical health are fine," I reply.

"Do you have any issues?"

Any issues? That question is like opening a can of worms in my brain. You could practically hear it pop. "My main issue is the screws' brutality," I tell Hazzard. "I was beaten up by the screws only half-an-hour after arriving on the ward, and the other patients are continually being assaulted by the screws. It's systematic and brutal and deliberate."

Hazzard shuffles some papers, more to look busy and important than to achieve anything. He gives a cough. "Yes, I see." He glances to the men either side of him. "I've investigated your complaint that you were beaten up by Charge Nurse Roach, Staff Nurse Flame and S.E.N. Dante, and I can find no evidence to support your allegation," he tells me.

I am doing my best to maintain my cool, but it is difficult under the circumstances. "That's cobblers," I snap, then draw a deep breath before continuing. "You must know about it," I protest. "Before breakfast the following day, the doctor who saw me when I arrived on the ward shook my hand and apologised for the attack. He apologised to me! So if a doctor who has nothing to do with my case was aware of it so soon, I'm pretty damn sure you would be too."

Hazzard replies without looking at me. "I can assure you I don't know about it."

I know I should remain cool, but his bold-faced lie rankles me. "Liar!" I snap. "You are a liar!"

The unknown male on my left speaks, so I turn my head to look at him. He's in his fifties, wears a short-sleeved white shirt with a cheap, nylon tie. His fingers are stained with nicotine. "Roger Clarke, nurse union rep," he says by way of introduction. "Do you think you should make such accusations against the nurses when you have no proof, Mr Ball?"

I give a deep sigh. "How can I have proof? They shut the door so there would be no witnesses."

Roach speaks, so I turn my head to the right. "We shut the door so that you could have some privacy whilst you were having your beard shaved off," he explains. "We do try to respect a patient's privacy."

"Rubbish, you shut the door because you didn't want the other patients to see me being assaulted," I reply.

Clarke speaks, so I turn my head to my left. I feel like I'm at Wimbledon. Fifteen love.

Clarke looks like he's struggling to keep up. "If you were assaulted, why didn't you have any cuts and bruises?"

"I had bruises on my body and testicles," I tell him, "but they were careful not to damage my face, to hit me anywhere that my injuries would be visible."

Roach speaks, and once more I turn my head to my right. Fifteen all. He has a serious look on his face. "So you're saying we've been specially taught to beat patients up without touching their faces?"

"No, of course not. Even a moron like you would be able to figure that out for yourself," I tell him.

Clarke speaks. Once more I turn my head to my left. "Then what are you saying?"

It's obvious that Clarke and Roach are making me keep on turning my head left and right to make me look stupid, so I ignore them and fix my gaze straight ahead on Hazzard. Not a pretty sight, but better than the Wimbledon back and forth I've been engaged in. "They assaulted me," I tell Hazzard.

Hazzard gulps, says, "I'm sure Mr Roach would never assault a patient."

I can see the look of fear in his eyes. "Look at you. You're scared, you're scared stiff of the screws. Are you afraid that if you criticise them they'll get the union on to you? Or maybe they'll beat you up too?"

"Really, Mr Ball," protests Hazzard.

Roach chips back in. "This is consistent with Ball's delusional and accusative behaviour," he tells Hazzard. "It's all in the daily notes, sir."

I stare at Roach. When did he become so polite?

"I think a change or increase in medication might be advisable," concludes Roach.

Hazzard nods sagely, as though this is a brilliant and original idea. "That's clearly something we should consider." He licks his lips, looks towards Roach, seeking approval.

I can't contain my disgust. "You're a coward, Hazzard!" "A spineless coward!"

Hazzard sits back in his seat, as though fearful that I might leap over the table and assault him.

"You're a bit overexcited, Ball," he says. Maybe you should

go outside and calm down?"

Roach stands up. The case conference is clearly over.

I rise from my seat, bend forward, look Hazzard straight in the eye and shout. "'You inadequate! You pathetic inadequate!"

Roach puts a restraining hand on my shoulder, but I'm done. Without another word, I march from the room.

The decision of the case conference is that I go to Dolphin High Security Ward and that my medication be changed to Largactil.

Chapter 9

Dolphin Ward has a familiar feel. Like the admissions ward, it is an 'L' shape, with the day room at the end of the long corridor and the dormitory at the end of the short corridor. Next to the bend of the 'L' on the short corridor is the ward office. The only difference with the admission ward is that there is no wooden board for the patients' locker keys. The patients keep their keys on them at all times.

The day room is divided in half by a glass and wooden partition, with one half housing a radio and TV, settees and chairs and tables, a shaving socket, and half the patients' lockers, while in the middle of the other half is a full-size snooker table. This side has more settees, tables and chairs, and the other half of the patients' lockers.

There are forty patients on Dolphin ward, and the usual charming collection of staff.

Each shift comprises four staff. I soon get to know the worst of them – Charge Nurse (Captain) Bligh, Staff Nurse Brill, and S.E.N. Pike. Brill is OK, Pike is an animal, but worst of all is Captain Bligh, who takes an immediate dislike to me.

On the principle of 'know thine enemy', I study Bligh. I'd guess him to be around forty -five, no more than 5ft 9ins tall, portly, with a plump face and a neatly trimmed moustache.

It soon becomes clear that he is a strict disciplinarian, who likes nothing more than shouting at a patient. He thinks he is firm but fair and is well-liked by the patients, but in reality, all the patients hate him, think he is a right bastard.

What I find most unsettling about Bligh is that he is sneakily violent, and psychologically vicious, he knows what to say to hurt people. Like all the staff he has access to the patients' files, which he clearly reads, searching for a patient's weakness, which he then uses to undermine and weaken them. I make a mental note to keep an eye on Bligh. If he is going to target me, well, it's only fair that I should do the same to him, right?

I quickly settle into the new routine. It's roughly the same as on the admission ward, except there is no afternoon work session and, before breakfast, the patients each scrub another patient's side room. Delightful.

After breakfast I'm assigned to cleaning the day room. I sweep then polish the parquet flooring, using an electric polisher. Much better than the decker we had on the Admissions ward.

I'm supposed to have help doing this, but my workmate, a psychopath known as Bruno, just stands talking to the day room screw, swapping stories about how they have beaten up some poor easy-going patient. To add insult to injury, Bruno gets paid a bonus each week for his so-called work, whereas I just get the basic.

Bonuses are based on a points system where the patients get marked out of 4. If a patient gets 4 points every day he gets a bonus. As well as being awarded points for work, the patients also get points for appearance and cooperation. While I always get 4 points for appearance, I typically get just 1 or 2 for cooperation.

One day, as I am vigorously decking the floor under the snooker table where the electric polisher cannot reach, the sweat dripping off me, Pike suddenly commands, "Ball! Go down and get me a cup of tea, two sugars."

I do as I am told, but on the way back from the kitchen I nip into the toilet and piss in the teacup. I continue on to the day room and place the tea on the table in front of Pike. He looks at the tea, looks at me suspiciously, says, "Why did you go in the toilet?"

Looking as innocent as possible, I say "Rail spilt some tea in the saucer so I went into the toilet to mop it up with the roller towel."

With my mission completed, I continue decking. After a short while, I look at Pike, who is ignoring the tea, and say, in a concerned manner, "Your tea is getting cold, sir, you'd better hurry up and drink it."

Pike gives me a look of abhorrence, "No. It's OK, I don't feel thirsty anymore."

I continue decking with a broad grin on my face, the screw staring at me with a look of pure hatred.

A short time later, Bligh strolls in. He and Pike chat, and Pike obviously tells Mr Bligh what happened. Bligh grins, commands me, "Ball! Go and get two cups of tea, both with two sugars."

Again, I do as I'm told.

Again, I go into the toilet and piss in the tea, but I only piss in one cup, remembering that the cup without the added ingredient is the one with flowers on it.

I set both cups on the table in front of the screws and continue my decking. After a brief period Bligh says, "Ball, you must be thirsty after all that decking, would you like a cup of tea." I pretend to be eternally grateful and go and pick up the cup with flowers on it and drink. When I've finished, I lick my lips and say, "Delicious", then resume my decking.

Bligh looks surprised, looks at the day room screw, shrugs his shoulders, picks up the other cup and starts drinking. He immediately gags and spits out the tea. I continue decking with a massive smile on my face and a look of absolute euphoria, studiously ignoring an incensed Bligh, who looks as though he is about to explode.

Round one to me…

My cleaning done, I slump into a chair in the day room.
"Whaddaya doin?"
I look up, am met by a strange sight, a patient dressed like a 1920s American gangster, with a double-breasted pinstripe suit, a wide tie, even a toothpick.

I'm reading a newspaper, so it would seem pretty self-evident what I'm doing.

The stranger sits down next to me, holds his hand out. "Name's Clive, but everyone calls me 'Evil C'. That's Clive spelled backwards," he explains.

I take the proffered handshake. "Ian," I reply, "but everyone calls me Ian."

"Your name's Ball, ain't that right?"

"Right."

"So how about I call you Ballsie, coz you look like you're kinda ballsie?"

"How about you call me Ian?"

Clive thinks about this for a minute. "Fair enough, Ian it is." He leans in closer. "The screws think I'm crazy," he confides.

I can't imagine why…

"But here's the thing," he tells me. "I ain't. It's all an act. I dress like this, pepper my speech with stuff like 'swim with the fishes', 'communion', 'confirmation', and it keeps the screws off my back. Then when I have my case conference, I tell the RMO they're all a bunch of rats and snitches, and that I can't tell them anything because of the omerta, the code of silence, well, they leave me alone for another three months."

"That's one strategy," I reply.

Clive leans in even closer. "You gotta figure out a way to game the system," he tells me. "You're new here, but you look like you're smart. It's all a big game to them, and just like in any game there's gonna be winners and losers. So which one you wanna be? You wanna be a patsy, a schmuck, and wind up swimming with the fishes, or you wanna be a boss, a capi?"

He directs my gaze around the ward. "See that loser over there?" There's a small mousy man sitting alone in the corner rocking back and forth. "You wanna be like him?"

As we watch, Bligh creeps up behind the mousy man, suddenly shouts, "Davis! How's the family?"

The mousy man, Davis, jumps at the sound of Bligh's voice, then resumes rocking even more frantically.

"Poor bastard burned his own house down, killed his wife and kid," Clive tells me. "The screws treat him like a punching bag, a play thing." He grips my arm. "So what's your angle? Who you gonna be? Coz believe me, if you don't decide, if you don't choose for yourself, then the screws will do it for you, capiche? And if they set the agenda, then you're a dead man, Ballsie, a dead man." He runs his finger across his throat for emphasis. "Next thing you know, you'll be wearing concrete boots and they'll be fishing your body out the Hudson River."

He stands up, straightens his tie, his cuffs. "See you around." And with that he struts off.

Despite his strange appearance, Clive's comments get me thinking. He's right. The screws run the ward, they set the tone, and they treat each of the patients differently depending on how the patients themselves behave. So am I going to be a victim? Someone to be bullied, like Davis, or am I going to write my own narrative, set my own agenda? It's an easy call to make. I decide to use my natural friendliness and good humour to do it. I thus set out to make friends with the other patients, giving them sweets and chocolates and writing letters for them.

Bligh quickly realises what I am doing, and sets out to turn me against the patients by running them down and criticising them, detailing all the reasons why I should dislike them or even avoid them, but when he does so I always defend them. When Bligh singles out an individual patient and details his bad points, I always counter with their good points.

Clive proves to be a good partner in crime in my dealings with the other patients. He has been there a while and knows everyone well, and in between his mafia speak fills me in on everyone's good and bad points, their quirks and foibles, things to say to them and things to avoid. I in return tell him jokes, which he seems to enjoy. So a typical conversation might go like this…

Clive sidles up to me, resplendent in his pinstripe suit. He looks around for a moment, then removes his toothpick before whispering to me. "You seen any bulls around this morning?"

I nod to Bligh, standing against the wall, surveying his domain and chewing on his moustache. "There's a gumshoe over there, but I don't think he's on to you."

Clive peers suspiciously at Bligh. "Yeah, I had him fingered for a dick." He pauses. "I got a shipment of hooch coming in later today, don't want any heat when the boys arrive."

"I'll watch your back," I say helpfully.

"I need a good lookout," says Clive, still staring at Bligh. "You scratch my back, I'll scratch yours, capiche?"

"Capiche."

"I can even set you up with a moll I know."

"You're too kind." I lean in like Clive, playing along. "Did I tell you, I was talking with doctor Hazzard yesterday? Doctor, I said to him, I keep getting the urge to purchase a big white bear from the Arctic. You know what he told me? You've got buy polar disorder!"

Clive snorts with laughter. "You crack me up, kid. Stick with me and I'll see that you're a made man one of these days."

"You know what that bastard Hazzard told me? He said that I have a preoccupation with vengeance. We'll see about that!"

Clive laughs some more, attracting Bligh's attention. He ambles over. "So what's so funny?" Like many impotent little bullies, Bligh is chronically insecure, assumes that people are laughing at him. He glares at me with his piggy little eyes, waiting for me to say the magic word, which for Bligh is 'Sir'. Bligh expects to be treated like a god, and as such, everybody must call him 'Sir'. Normally, if a patient delays for a moment when calling him sir, Bligh will give him a hefty slap across the chops, but I have a variety of techniques to avoid doing so.

I look up at him. "Well s-s-s-s-s-s-s – "

I can see him waiting for it, almost twitching with impatience.

"Well s-s-s-s-s-s-s-s-s-s-" I really string it out. "Well s-s-s-s-s-s-"

"Spit is out man!" he roars.

I look at Clive. "Well, s-s-s-s-shit, I forgot what I was going to say."

"Idiot!" Bligh glares at me. "I've seen puddles with more intelligence than you Ball!"

"Yes, s-s-s-s-s-s-s-s-"

Bligh has had enough, toddles away, leaving me and Clive in peace once more.

"As you said, a dick," I whisper to Clive, who dissolves into a fit of giggles.

Despite having my first diary stolen, I resume my writing. The more time I spend in Rampton, the more determined I become to get a public enquiry into the screws' brutality. I thus keep notes myself on the various incidents I witness, and also take steps to prepare the patients to act as witnesses in the court actions against the screws that will take place as a result of the public enquiry.

I thus spend time drumming it into the other patients' heads that they should go over and over again in their minds the day and date of any assault they have witnessed, including the exact time, the names of the screws who committed the assault, the name of the patient who was assaulted and the names of the other witnesses.

If they do this, I tell them, they will get the details of the assault firmly fixed in their mind and they will be unshakeable when subjected to the ferocious questioning of the defence barrister, who will try to confuse them and make them appear to be an unreliable witness.

I also stress to the other patients that they should keep what they have witnessed to themselves and not confer with the other patients. Thus the defence barrister will be unable to say that the patients are conspiring against the screws. I stress that they should keep to the facts and not exaggerate or embellish them, which they might be tempted to do to strengthen their case.

It is a warm summer's day, and the windows are open, which is a welcome change as the day room is often quite stuffy, and not all the patients have good personal hygiene.

As I sit writing, a large fly buzzes past, then jags back and tries to settle on my arm. I wave my arm and it flies away, but instead of buzzing off and annoying another patient, it circles round and comes in for another landing, this time on my face. Again I swat it away, but again it returns.

Exasperated, I set my pen and notepad down, observe the fly for a moment. It is still hovering around me. Fine, if that's what you want…

I stand up calmly, observe the fly for a short while then, in a lightning move, headbutt it. Much to my surprise I make contact, and the dazed fly spirals down to the floor, landing at my foot. I look at it for a moment, but it seems to be out for the count.

I raise and lower my arm in true boxing referee style and count it out – one, two, three, four, five, six, seven, eight, nine, ten – then cross my hands over each other and shout, "Out!"

Triumphant, I raise my arms over my head, clasp my hands together, shake them and exclaim, "Yes! The winner!" Then calmly sit down and resumed writing.

Staff Nurse Brill, who has watched the whole performance, strolls over. "Ball? You crack me up."

I smile. "Anything to get through the day," I tell him.

Unlike the other screws, Brill has a sense of humour. He also has a large, bald head and a thick, red, bushy beard. "You must have put a double dose on today, Baldy," I tell him. "I can smell you from here."

Brill applies copious amounts of hair restorer to his bald dome each day in a vain attempt to stimulate some hair growth, and you can smell it from halfway across the day room.

"I think it's helping," he says optimistically as he strokes his shiny head.

"I've seen more hair on a billiard ball," I tell him.

Brill laughs. "Do you have any good jokes today?" he asks.

"Jokes I have," I tell him, "but I can't guarantee the quality."

"Go on. Give me your best shot."

I think for a moment. "I heard that my 13-year-old niece is

already taking heroin," I tell him. "It's amazing how fast they shoot up these days."

Brill laughs. "Not bad, six out of ten."

"OK, how about this one. When I was a kid, my father used to hit me with a camera. I still get flashbacks."

"Better, seven out of ten." He stands up. "But don't give up the day job just yet."

"Everyone's a critic," I tell him as he strolls away.

Just at that moment I hear the sound of Pike's angry voice from the corridor, the sound of a slap as his hand hits a patient's face. Moments later a patient stumbles into the day room, his face red and blotchy, a reminder that despite the efforts of Brill, the general atmosphere of the ward is poisonous, with the majority of the screws continually verbally and physically abusing the patients, whether it is by shouting at the patients, barking orders, issuing insults and threats, handing out extra work or physically abusing them. The atmosphere only becomes more relaxed after seven o'clock at night, when the night shift check in. For some reason they are less abusive than the day shift, allowing the patients some respite.

Chapter 10

After several months in Rampton I decide that it is time to reveal to everyone that the incident involving Princess Anne was not a real kidnap attempt, but rather, an elaborate hoax executed with the help of an old friend in the police force, Frank.

I have waited several months for Frank to step forward and explain what happened, detailing his involvement, but to my surprise, Frank has remained silent, forcing me to reveal the nature and extent of the hoax myself.

In addition, the beating I received on arriving at Rampton has influenced my decision to wait six months, instead of the intended two weeks, to reveal that it was all a hoax.

As I noted, before they administered the beating, the screws shut the cell door so there were no witnesses, making it impossible for the police to be able to prosecute the assailants for assault.

I am determined that the screws won't get away with this, and thus decide to stay in Rampton a little longer than anticipated and collect evidence of other assaults committed by my assailants to ensure they can be prosecuted for these assaults and sent to prison. However, I have now collated enough evidence to support a prosecution of the offending screws, and am thus ready to get out of Rampton as soon as possible.

The gist of the hoax is that Frank had taken the gunpowder out of the bullets, so that I couldn't have shot anyone and, therefore, couldn't be guilty of attempted murder, and he had also substituted another woman for Princess Anne, so I couldn't be guilty of attempting to kidnap her. However, in order to prove my innocence I need Frank to step forward and reveal his part in the prank.

I therefore write to Frank, telling him that I know it was a hoax, and asking him to get me out of Rampton. I send the letter to Uxbridge Police Station as Frank was a Detective Constable stationed there. Each day I wait eagerly to hear from Frank – a letter, a phone call, even a visit – but after two weeks have heard nothing.

I assume that Frank is no longer working there, so I write to the Station Sergeant and ask him to put a notice on the station notice board, offering a £50 reward to anyone who knows Frank and who will get in touch with him and ask him to contact me.

Much to my frustration, after a further two weeks I have still heard nothing. It is time for another course of action. If Frank is not prepared to step forward and admit his role on the matter, I will have to make it public. I therefore write explaining how the incident was a hoax to solicitors, MPs, The National Council For Civil Liberties, the British national newspapers and relevant local newspapers – all in all about 50 letters. Surely I will get a response now?

When a further month passes without a single response, it is clear that something – or somebody – is obstructing my attempts to reveal the truth.

Hazzard.

At my next meeting with him, I confront him about it.

"I've written a lot of letters recently," I begin, calm and collected.

"That's very good, Ball," replies Hazzard. "Letter writing is a good hobby, it keeps you in touch with the world, don't you think?"

Do I detect the hint of a smirk as he replies? "The funny thing is," I continue, "no one has replied to me. Over fifty letters sent in the last six weeks, and not a single response. Don't you find that rather curious?"

"Maybe you gave the wrong return address?"

Definitely a smirk this time.

Bligh, who is standing watch in the corner of the room, joins in. "Or maybe, Ball, your letters were so idiotic that no one wanted to reply to you?"

I ignore him, keep my attention on Hazzard. "I don't think that's the case," I tell him. "I think that someone is stopping my letters, blocking them from ever getting out."

Hazzard tugs at his scruffy tie, rubs his nose, two clear 'tells' that he is about to start lying. "I can't imagine who would do that, or why," he replies.

"You are blocking my letters," I accuse, "to stop the truth getting out about why I'm here, and to stop my calls for a public enquiry into the abuse here."

Bligh snorts with laughter. "As I put in my daily reports, sir, the patient remains delusional and accusative." He gives a little cough. "Time to up his meds, methinks."

Hazzard continues to bluster. "Maybe your letters got lost in the post? Did you put stamps on them?"

I'm trying to remain calm, but it's hard. "Of course I put stamps on them! And it would stretch plausibility to think that fifty letters all got 'lost', especially as six of the letters were to my mother asking her to come to visit me. What are the chances of six letters to the same address all getting lost in the post?"

Hazzard tries again. "Maybe people are just slow in responding?"

"No! Had my mother received the letters, she would have undoubtedly replied. Five months previously she sent me a food parcel, and enclosed a letter in which she said she desperately wanted to visit me." I glare at Hazzard. "There is one, and only one plausible explanation. You are blocking my letters! You are nothing more than a common vicious criminal, guilty of the crime of conspiracy to pervert the course of justice."

Hazzard glances at Bligh, then looks at me with a weak smile on his face. "Conspiracy to pervert the course of justice? What do you mean?"

"You know exactly what I mean! You've read the letters. I shouldn't be here. It was all a hoax, and if my letters are allowed to get through to the recipients, I will be able to get the evidence to prove it was a hoax and be released, which, believe me, would be a lot less stressful for all of us."

"Yes, well…" Hazzard looks at his watch as though, like the rabbit in Alice in Wonderland, he has somewhere urgent to get to. "We'll pick this up again next week."

Bligh coughs to get his attention.

"Oh, yes, and I do think we should have another look at your medication levels."

And that's it. A stonewall response, and more medication. Always the medication.

The use of medication is pervasive in Rampton, a form of slow torture to calm and control the patients, with no one to appeal to if you don't agree with the diagnosis or the treatment. At various times I am given different psychotropic drugs, all of which have wide ranging and disruptive side-effects including fever, blurred vision, restlessness, muscle spasms, headaches, shakes, constipation, lethargy, drowsiness and a befogged brain.

There is no doubt in my mind that I am being subjected to the drug torture in an effort to break me and make me recant my beliefs, but I refuse to be cowed by their abuse. Instead, I continue with my Plan A, to try and send letters relevant to the hoax, and also come up with a Plan B – writing an autobiography. If I can't prove my innocence by sending letters, I shall prove it by publishing my autobiography.

This seems only logical, as there must have been a lot of ordinary members of the public in The Mall who witnessed the hoax. In order for the truth to be concealed, Frank would have had to persuade these people not to say anything by telling them that if I didn't know it was a hoax, I am obviously a very dangerous man because I would have thought I had live bullets in my gun and that I had actually shot those people. I would therefore have been guilty of the very serious offences of attempted murder and attempted kidnapping and should be locked up.

Furthermore, Frank would have also explained that it was

to my advantage to be locked up because it would save my life. Frank believed that he was saving my life because I had previously told him that I would commit suicide if I could not get married and that I couldn't get married because I was too weak and inadequate to form a relationship with a woman. So it would be better for me if I were locked up, away from women.

However, if I can publish my autobiography I will be able to show that I wasn't inadequate, and that I knew all along that it was a hoax. The public would thus see that they had been hoodwinked, that I was a sane, innocent man, and that the authorities should release me.

Buoyed by the possibilities offered by the completion of my autobiography, I increase and expand my letter writing, sending letters to MPs, solicitors, barristers, newspapers, TV stations, civil liberty organisations, the CCRC, and book publishers. Following my confrontation with Hazzard, it becomes clear that at least some of my letters are now escaping the confines of the hospital, as I now start receiving some replies. Although the replies I do receive offer no hope, and even pour scorn on my hypothesis, I remain undaunted and continue my letter-writing campaign.

Needless to say, all this activity on my part is met with resistance by Hazzard and Bligh. At first I think it will be confined to the usual – changes to my medication to slow me down and confuse me, and more insults and abuse from Bligh, but one morning they increase the stakes dramatically.

I have just got out of bed when Bligh appears in the doorway with three orderlies in his wake. "Morning Ball!" He seems in a suspiciously good mood.

I glance at the orderlies arrayed behind him. "What's all this?"

Bligh gives an evil grin. "ECT."

Those three letters send chills through me. ECT means electroconvulsive therapy, the application of massive electric shocks to the brain, and is typically used for patients with highly severe, psychotic or suicidal depression. However, at Rampton it is also used as a form of control or punishment for difficult or problematic patients. Clearly, my extensive letter writing has put me into that category.

"I don't want ECT," I protest.

Bligh is loving this. "Mister Ball doesn't want it, eh? So are we now the doctor, who knows what's best for the patients?"

"I might not know what's best for the patients," I point out, "but I do know what's best for me, and it's definitely not ECT."

One of the side effects of ECT is a loss of swathes of both short term and long-term memory, which would be disastrous for my attempts to catalogue the abuses I have seen at Rampton. One patient has told me that after his first session of ECT, his family had visited him for two hours, yet when they visited again two weeks later they found that he had no memory at all of the previous visit.

Bligh is unimpressed by my protests. He preens his bushy moustache. "I haven't had my breakfast yet, so let's not dilly-dally." He gives a nod, and the orderlies, all burly individuals with enough strength to subdue a rowdy rhinoceros, grab me and begin to haul me from the room.

I wriggle, squirm, drag my feet, but it makes no difference, I am hauled out of my room and along the corridor towards the treatment room. Bligh ambles along behind making small talk. "I'm having the full English today," he informs me, "with extra sausage." He leers at me. "You're probably the kind who likes an extra sausage from time to time, aren't you, Ball?"

For once I have no witty reply.

We reach the treatment room and Bligh opens the door, ushers us in. The orderlies lift me effortlessly onto a table, strap my ankles, wrist, and forehead. I can't turn my head, just gaze upwards at the harsh fluorescent lights. Doctor Hazzard appears above me, close enough to see the tufts of hair he missed when he shaved that morning, smell the halitosis on his breath. I should have guessed he'd have bad breath. "Good morning, Ball."

"What's so good about it?" I reply.

Hazzard grins. "Because it's time for your ECT," he tells me. "ECT means Electroconvulsive Therapy," he explains, "and involves sending electric shocks through your brain to trigger a seizure."

"I know what the hell it is," I growl, "but why am I having it?"

"Because I have prescribed it for you," he answers breezily.

"And why have you prescribed it for me?" I persist.

"Because I'm your doctor," he replies. "And I know what's best for you."

"That's a tautological argument," I point out, but Hazzard is unimpressed. He has me exactly where he wants me, and nothing is going to dampen his good mood. As we talk he is affixing electrodes to the side of my head. "You won't feel a thing. I'll give you a muscle relaxant before we start, and you'll be under a general anaesthetic the whole time."

The anaesthetist waves from above my head.

As Hazzard continues to prepare me for the treatment, Bligh leans in so close that I can feel his moustache tickle my ear when he speaks. "If I had my way we would skip the muscle relaxant and the general anaesthetic."

Hazzard gives a little laugh. "Now now, Mr Bligh, none of your little jokes."

Bligh straightens up. "He thinks I'm joking…"

Hazzard has finally finished fiddling around with the electrodes. He peers at me. "Any last questions before we begin?"

"I know what you're doing," I tell him. "But you won't silence me. I am innocent, and I aim to prove it."

Bligh gives a deep sigh of irritation. "Can we get the fuck on with this? My breakfast is waiting?"

And those are the last words I hear before the anaesthetist clamps the mask over my face and turns on the gas. "Can we get the fuck on with this? My breakfast is waiting?" Words to live by.

Chapter 11

After my ECT, things return to their usual pattern. Bligh works hard to make my life as miserable as possible, while I continue my campaigns and do my best to get up Bligh's overly hairy nose. Does the ECT affect my memory? It's hard to say. How do you remember if you've forgotten something? It's like when you've lost something, and someone says, "where did you last have it." If I knew that it wouldn't be lost! However, the fact that I remember the ECT so clearly, and am able to recall the events and write this book, suggests that I have escaped the worst effects of the ECT. I think Bligh knows it too, because his campaign against me becomes even more personal after the ECT.

"All right, Ball, that's long enough."

I am seated on the toilet, doing what must be done, and in no mood to be hurried. This is almost a sacred time because sitting on the toilet is one of the few times during the day that a patient can be alone and unobserved. "What do you mean, long enough?" I reply. "I haven't finished."

I hear Bligh's heavy footsteps approach, then a loud rap on the door. "You've been in there six minutes," he informs me. "Your time's up."

"There's no time limit for sitting on the toilet," I protest.

"There is for you," he tells me, "and your time is up." He begins rapping furiously on the door. "Come on out, Ball! Come on out!"

"Make me, you fat poofter," I retort.

"If I have to get you out, it won't be pretty," Bligh warns me.

"You get out," I retort, "you make the place smell. Next to you a skunk smells sweet."

"Right, that's it!" Blusters Bligh.

At which point I stand up, flush the toilet, and open the door. "Were you saying something?"

Bligh glares at me for a moment, then storms off. "You'll pay for this," he warns as he leaves.

Shortly thereafter I have an interview with Hazzard that helps to make sense of some aspects of my stay in Rampton that have been bothering me.

As usual, Bligh is standing watch in the corner of the room, but unusually, Hazzard seems very happy, almost giddy, with a sickly smile plastered to his face. "Ball! Lovely to see you," he says as I sit down.

I am immediately suspicious, but say nothing.

"How are you?" he begins.

Still puzzled by his false bonhomie, I answer in a neutral fashion. "I'm fine"

"I'll jump straight into it," he says. "Have you noticed that time used to go quickly but now it goes very slowly?"

What a curious question... But I think about it..."Yes, I suppose it does."

Hazzard grins again, sweeps his thinning hair back. "I'll try to explain. For the past two years, time has been going twice as fast as normal."

I frown. "That's impossible, if time was going twice as fast, when it was night-time outside it would be day-time in here, so you would have to have a false sun, which is obviously impossible."

Hazzard gives Bligh a conspiratorial look. "Have you heard of the new Halogen lamps, how bright they are?"

"Of course."

"And when you have been out in the exercise yard have you noticed that the sun stays in the same place and never moves?"

Awareness begins to grow in my mind. "Yes, I did notice that. Also, I used to study the sun for five or six minutes at a time, and I wondered why the edges were smooth."

"Exactly," declares Hazzard triumphantly. "And didn't you wonder how you could look into the sun for five minutes when, normally, this would have blinded you?"

I nod slowly. "I should have realised there was something wrong." The more I think about it, the more it makes sense. "There was a time when I was on the admission ward and a patient was trying to light a cigarette using his glasses as a magnifying glass to concentrate the sun's rays on the tip," I tell Hazzard. "It didn't work. I wondered why it didn't work, it should have."

"Further proof it was a false sun," adds Hazzard.

"There is another thing that supports your theory," I admit. "When I was on the admission ward I noticed that time seemed to be going very fast. I thought there was something wrong with my watch so I tested it by counting the seconds up to one minute by saying, 'One Mississippi, two Mississippi,' then checking against the watch. Sure enough, one minute of counting equalled two minutes on the watch. At the time I thought there was something wrong with the watch, and sent it in for repair. And now it seems that time was going twice as fast as normal… But why would anyone do that?"

Hazzard licks his lips, leans forward. "It's because when you were outside you were living one year behind everybody else, so we had to speed up time to make up the missing year."

This is deeply puzzling. I think for a moment, then say, "So you're saying that, in fact, the 'offence' took place on the 20th March 1975 and not the 20th March 1974."

"Yes. That's correct."

"Why was I living one year behind?"

Hazzard has a concerned look on his face. "Frank did it to save your life, to prevent you from committing suicide."

"Why the hell would I commit suicide?" I protest.

"Because when you were younger, you told Frank that you desperately wanted to get married, and that if you weren't married by the time you were twenty-five you would commit suicide. So, to stop you committing suicide, just before your twenty-fifth birthday, in 1972, Frank convinced you it was 1971 and that you were one year younger. That way he had an extra year in which to make sure you didn't take your own life."

I say nothing, trying to make sense of it all.

"It obviously worked," concludes Hazzard, "because you're still alive."

My mind is in a whirl. "I see," is the only reply I can muster.

Like a switch being clicked, Hazzard's whole demeanour changes. He snaps my file shut, folds his hands in front of him, smiles at me like nothing has happened, like the whole conversation hasn't taken place. "Well I think we're done here." He nods to Bligh, who gives me a nudge to get me moving.

My mind still in a daze, I stand up, wander back to the day room, sit down and gaze into space.

I have no idea how long I sit like that, am finally interrupted by Bligh shouting at me. "Ball! Ball!"

I look up.

"Are you going to sit there all day like a brainless cabbage?"

"No, no, I just…" I look at Bligh. He was there. He heard what Hazzard said. "My interview with Hazzard?"

"What about it? Waste of time on a moron like you if you ask me."

"What he said about time going twice as fast as normal? Were you in on that from the start?"

Bligh frowns at me. "What are you drivelling on about now?"

"What Doctor Hazzard said. About time going twice as fast as normal for me."

Bligh shakes his head, lets out a whistle of despair through his moustache. "I told him."

"Told who what?"

"I told Hazzard you were losing it, but he didn't listen to me."

"But this morning, the meeting?"

"You're clearly having a psychotic breakdown. I'm going to recommend to Hazzard that he prescribe the appropriate medication for you." A big smile creases his face. "Looks like it's Stelazine for you, my boy!" And with that he struts away, the smile never leaving his face.

Chapter 12

Stelazine. It's wonderful stuff, you really should try it. Doctors use it to treat certain mental or mood disorders such as schizophrenia or psychotic disorders, on the theory that it can help you think more clearly, feel less nervous, and take part in everyday life. It can also reduce aggressive behaviour and the desire to hurt yourself or others. However, at Rampton it is given out like cough sweets, with its common side effects of far more interest to the staff than its supposed benefits. The biggest of these, drowsiness, makes the screws' job easier, as it creates a docile, drugged population of inmates.

I also find that it makes me feel dizzy and anxious, and gives me constant headaches. But through the drug-induced fog, I am clear-headed enough to know that I have to get out of Rampton and into Broadmoor. It will be a lot better there. The superintendent, Dr McGrath, is a good man who won't stop my letters or adverts in the newspapers, whether they be domestic or foreign, local or national, which will ultimately enable me to find people who knew of my Local Wag identity, the identity given me by the newspapers when they reported the practical jokes Frank and myself played on the general public in and around my hometown of Uxbridge. I will also be able to find people who knew I was living one year behind everybody else, which is the key to me exposing the truth and finally achieving my freedom.

Having come up with a plan, I now have to find a way to make it happen, and given the degree of control that they have over my life, that has to mean making Hazzard and Bligh push for my transfer. As I drift off to sleep I begin to formulate a plan to make each of them, in their own way, want me gone.

I start to put my plan into effect the next day when Bligh calls me into the office on some trivial matter. "Ball!" he rasps.

I totter over, stand at the office door.

"Do you want me, sir?"

He looks up from his paperwork.

"Yes, yes, come here."

I stand in the doorway. "Is that Ball? BA double L?"

"Yes, of course!" He is getting frustrated.

"Ball, B………A………L………L, Ball?" I ask again.

I can see his pale face turning puce. "Yes!" he screams. "B…………………………A…………………………L……… ………………L. Would you like me to write it down you cretin?"

I immediately turn into the very personification of helpfulness. "No indeed, sir, no need, I'm here right now. What was it you wanted?"

His eyes bore into me with hatred.

Later that day I initiate another strand of my campaign. Bligh has a distinct body odour and has been very self-conscious about it as I am always making sly comments about the awful smell whenever he is around. As I stand talking with Clive in the day room, I see a reflection in the window – Bligh is approaching me from behind. Clive is engaged in his usual mafia inspired schtick, dressed from head to toe like the Godfather. "So I says to him, you cross me again and you'll be swimming with the fishes, know what I mean?"

I interrupt him. "What is that awful smell, Don Clive? Have you buried one of your enemies in here?"

Clive scowls. "Me? No. I don't shit where I eat, capiche?"

Bligh is almost upon us, well within hearing range. "Well something in here smells awful, and the smell is getting stronger."

Bligh is right behind me. I can almost feel his rage. I turn quickly. "Oh, Mister Bligh, it's you. What a surprise."

The look on Bligh's face is a picture as he fights to maintain his calm.

I cover my face with my hand as though blocking out a foul smell. "We were just talking about – "

He cuts me off, his beady eyes boring into me with a look of pure hatred. "I don't give a damn what you were talking about." He nods to Clive. "Time for your session."

Clive gives me a wink as he follows Bligh back across the room. "Don't worry, they won't get nothin' out of me. And keep an eye out for that moll I told you about, she's a real kitty cat, know what I mean?"

And with that they are gone.

A few days later I find another opportunity to get up Bligh's hairy nose. Whenever a group of outside visitors come on the ward to have a look around, the screws desperately try to make out that Rampton is a hospital and the screws are nurses by putting on white coats.

As a group of visitors in suits and ties are being shown around the ward, I march up to Bligh, resplendent in his immaculate snow white coat, and says, "Two choc ices please."

Bligh glares at me for a long moment, then forces out a fake laugh. "Ball, you are so funny."

I know he will get back at me for it later, but just at that moment, it is worth it.

I also have a plan for Hazzard, but before I can put it into effect I am summoned for another meeting with him, one which leaves me reeling for several weeks.

As usual, Hazzard sits behind his desk in his scruffy jacket and poorly knotted tie, but today he has a big smile on his face. Bligh lurks in the corner, and he too seems unusually cheerful as he looks at me.

"Hello, how are you?" begins Hazzard. He smiles at me, gives a quick glance towards Bligh.

"I'm fine," I say slowly. What is going on?

"After I saw you last month, Frank and I put our heads together, and we have decided to tell you what is going on."

"You and Frank are having discussions about me?" I gasp. After months of denying that he has ever met Frank, Hazzard is now admitting to speaking with him. He makes it sound like they have become best friends.

"Oh yes," replies Hazzard breezily. "We have spoken numerous times. Lovely chap, isn't he?"

I glance at Bligh. He is grinning like a simpleton, positively revelling in my astonishment and discomfort.

This is a fantastic revelation, not only has Hazzard acknowledged meeting Frank, but now admits that he talks to him regularly about me,

"Anyway, what I really wanted to talk to you about today is your powers."

"My powers?" I feel like Alice, plunging down the rabbit hole. How deep will it go before I hit the bottom?

"Yes. You have ESP – Extra Sensory Powers."

"I do?"

Again Hazzard glances at Bligh before replying. "Oh yes, quite remarkable powers.

But, whenever you use your psychic powers you repress it into your subconscious mind so you can't remember what you have done."

What he is saying makes sense in some warped way.

"You are unique, nobody can do what you can do," continues Hazzard, cheerily.

"What can I do?"

"Well, let's see. So far you have healed people, brought people back from the dead, made yourself invisible, teleported yourself and others, turned women's bodies back so that they are young and beautiful and can live forever, given people genius IQs of 160 and photographic memories…" He looks up at Bligh. "Have I missed anything?"

"He can also read people's minds," Bligh reminds him.

"Oh yes, shouldn't forget that one. Rather handy I would imagine," he grins.

I sit in stunned silence, trying to process this. Is it a joke? Are

Hazzard and Bligh just messing with me, or are they serious?

Hazzard can see my doubts. "I know you will find all this ridiculous and you won't believe me," he tells me, "but we intend to build up your self-confidence so that you can gradually bring the memories of what you have done from your subconscious to your conscious mind, which will unlock your powers."

I glance at Bligh. Good luck with that, I think. Bligh and the other screws spend their entire time trying to destroy the inmates' self-confidence in order to make them docile and easy to control.

"Whereas, at the moment," continues Hazzard, "you can only use your powers when you are acting subconsciously, once we have built up your self-confidence you will be able to use them consciously. This will mean you will be able to turn your own body back, be young and handsome, and find a girl and get married."

I scowl. Is he serious?

Hazzard rattles on, clearly warming to his task. "You will also be able to use your gifts to benefit mankind," he explained. "For example, you can cure everybody in the world of an illness all at once, instantly. We have already done an experiment to prove you can do this. We put half a dozen sick people in different countries situated throughout the world and we asked you to cure them. You sent a blast of psychic energy that engulfed the whole world, and the people were all instantly cured."

I shake my head to clear the cobwebs. "I don't remember any of this," I admit.

Hazzard waves my protests aside. "You will, in time. You just have to relax, trust the process, and wait for it to happen, and in the end your stay here will greatly benefit yourself and everybody else."

I finally manage to frame a coherent thought. "Why would I suppress something like this?"

"Self-defence," replies Hazzard breezily.

"Explain, please."

Hazzard momentarily adopts a more serious air. "You think

we don't know your beliefs, your agenda?"

Bligh gives a snort of derision.

"Despite Mr Bligh's disbelief, it is clear to me that you are an exceptionally dangerous working-class dissenter. If you had used your psychic powers to help people, you would have been championed internationally, and would have been able to use this world-wide support to transform Britain into a fair and democratic society. Clearly, the authorities couldn't have allowed that to happen, which you knew. You therefore suppressed your powers so that the authorities didn't have you murdered."

I had to admit there was a certain logic to that, and he was certainly correct when it came to my views.

"The British upper-class authorities are obviously terrified of the threat you could pose to their luxurious way of living, so they would have silenced you permanently by murdering you. So don't you see, by suppressing it, you are outsmarting the authorities because, although you are locked up, you can still write letters promoting your dissenting philosophies, thereby transforming society."

I nod slowly in silent agreement.

"There, you see, it all makes sense, doesn't it?"

Hazzard's beaming smile is making me feel slightly nauseous.

He folds his hands in front of him. "That's it, that's all I have to say," he concludes.

I sit staring at him, unable to form anything coherent to say.

Bligh steps over, gives me a nudge. "Let's get moving, Ball. Some of us have things to do."

Still in a daze, I climb to my feet.

And then Hazzard delivers the kicker. "Of course, you won't remember any of this conversation," he tells me. He smiles again. "You will repress it into your subconscious, as you repress all conversations even remotely connected with the ESP."

I stare at him.

"These include when you are cheeky when talking to the staff, because you were very cheeky when talking to Frank about the ESP."

Bligh gives me a nudge and I stumble towards the door.

"I hope you progress well with your treatment," chirps Hazzard as I step outside into the corridor.

I go to the day room and plonk myself down in front of the television. The screen flickers, the sound blares, but I take no notice, I am in a world of my own, my mind in a whirl. Despite what Hazzard said, I find that I can recall the entire conversation. I begin to try and process it logically.

Point one – Hazzard says I've got ESP. Bullshit! I'm a practical, down to earth person, I'm nothing like the other-worldly types who say they've got ESP. But perhaps that's a mark of someone who truly does have ESP? They don't boast about it, or try and make themselves seem like something they aren't, they just quietly use their powers?

Then what of my powers?

Hazzard said I can teleport myself. Surely, if I were in one place one moment and in another place a split second later, I would wonder how the hell I got there. That has never happened to me, so scratch that from the list.

He also said I've got powers of healing. Surely I would have cured myself when I had some ailment, such as the flu? I think about this for a moment. It's true that when I go to bed with a headache, I can think positive thoughts and the headache goes. But surely this is just the power of positive thought, has nothing to do with ESP? Anyone who is a positive thinker can do it, right?

He also said that I can heal the entire population of the world in an instant. That is clearly absolute codswallop. In fact, the more I think about it, the more I decide it's all rubbish.

So what was it all about? I think our friend Hazzard is playing mind games. He's probably hoping I will go around telling everybody I've got ESP. He can then say I'm mad and up my medication. He's trying to find an excuse to give me so many drugs that I can't think straight. The bastard. But I'll beat him. I'll make sure I never mention anything he said.

I stare out the window at a dull, rainy day, my mind still processing. It seems clear to me that Hazzard was getting pleasure out of demonstrating that he knows something that I didn't know, but, being a weak vindictive man, he would have got more pleasure out of seeing my distress than from imparting the information.

And hearing this I would undoubtedly be extremely distressed because I would know that, if the information were true, it would mean I was going to spend the rest of my life in Rampton. I would never get out.

And yet there is a grain of truth in what he said – he admitted to meeting Frank for the first time. More controlling behaviour from Hazzard. In his official reports he says that I am delusional, have an imaginary friend, Frank, who I blame for the kidnapping, but in person, Hazzard admits to me that he knows Frank and has spoken to him, probably several times if he has this level of information about me. Bastard.

It's time to up my campaign against both Hazzard and Bligh. I smile as I realise that I can use these new developments to have some sport. For example, I can say what I like to Captain Bligh – I can call him a fat slob, a poofter, a cretin – and there's nothing he can do about it, they'll have to say I'm talking subconsciously.

I lean back in my seat, fold my hands across my stomach. They want to play mind games? Fine. Two can play that game…

Chapter 13

I happily spend the next few weeks slyly digging at Bligh, then pleading ignorance every time he calls me on it, and sure enough, I am summoned to Hazzard's office a few weeks later to be told I am due for another case conference to discuss my progress.

Normally, I would sit there berating the RMO, the screws and the system, the natural reaction of anyone who has to deal with these psychopathic morons on a daily basis. However, I have come to realise that were I to do this, it would have no effect on them because they are used to being berated by the patients. It would be like water off a duck's back, as they would just take it all in their stride.

I decide that it would have much more impact if I make a mockery of the whole proceedings, acting in a jocular manner, making jokes and wisecracks and generally taking the piss. I am certain that this will enrage Hazzard and Bligh, neither of whom has the ability to take personal insults due to their inherent weakness.

And the beauty of this plan? They can't do anything about it, can't punish me, because they have told me that I say and do things subconsciously.

The case conference takes place in Dolphin Ward's dining room.

I knock lightly on the door, ready to put my plan into effect, working to keep the grin of anticipation from my face.

After a moment, a terse, impatient, "Yes!" comes from within.

I open the door, enter the room and walk towards a solitary

chair positioned alone in the centre of the room. This layout is designed for maximum intimidation, but today I am immune.

"Sit!" commands Hazzard.

For a moment I continue to stand in front of the chair, facing the RMO, then slowly sink to the floor until I am on my knees.

Hazzard gazes at me with a weary expression. "What are you doing, Ball?"

What am I doing? I'm just getting started I think. I kneel on the floor, my body at attention, bend my arms at the elbow and raise my forearms, relax my wrists and let my hands hang down limply.

As Hazzard stares at me in incredulity, I open my mouth, let my tongue loll out, and start panting. I look just like a dog who has been told to sit up and beg and is patiently waiting for praise from his master.

Hazzard looks both quizzical and annoyed. "What are you doing?" he demands.

I pant a few more times, then explain. "The way you told me to sit was like a master telling his dog to sit, so I thought that if you were going to treat me like an animal I would behave like one. Sir."

He observes me with disgust for a moment, then shouts, "Get up!"

I laboriously raise my body from the floor and plonk my arse on the chair, with a loud sigh.

There is a brief period of silence as Hazzard flicks through my notes before he says, "How are you?" He is trying to sound sincere, but failing miserably.

"I'm fine. It's just that I keep on seeing spots in front of my eyes," I tell him.

Hazzard frowns. "Have you seen a doctor?"

"No," I reply quickly, "just spots." I smile benignly. "But I'll let you know if I see a doctor."

Hazzard gives me a look that manages to contain surprise, annoyance and disgust all in one glance, but persists with his normal line of questions. "How's your mental health?"

"Well, I used to be schizophrenic but we're alright now," I reply quickly, looking around the room.

To my left, wearing a happy smile, is a female uniformed screw. Based on her uniform I surmise that she is a higher-up screw, senior to Mr Bligh. She's also middle -aged, ugly, with a moustache and hairy legs – the antidote to desire. As she looks like a Bavarian milkmaid, I decide to nickname her 'Gerta'.

Straight ahead of me is RMO Hazzard.

Several feet to the right of Hazzard, sitting on the corner, are two, youngish, males. They have no connection with me whatsoever and are obviously there just to make up the numbers. I nickname them 'Pinky and Perky' They are smiling, seem to be enjoying themselves. I love an appreciative audience, so smile back at them.

A few feet away from them, sitting on a table that runs along the right side of the room, is Staff Nurse Brill. He has his head down, studying the top of the table with a faint, guilty, smile on his face, like a schoolboy who is trying, and failing, to stifle a laugh.

Directly to my right is the miserable countenance of Mr Bligh, who is clearly not enjoying my performance. Seeing his expression encourages me to continue with my tactic.

"My main problem is that I have an inferiority complex," I tell Hazzard. "Admittedly it's not a very good one, but it's the best I can manage."

Hazzard looks up, as though he is about to say something, but I plough on, giving him no space to interject. "I suppose in truth, it's not actually a complex, as I really am inferior. It's all down to my small penis." I look down at my lap. "Percy, as I call it, is so small that when I was younger, the girls named me 'Justin'."

"Ball?" interrupts Hazzard, but I ignore him.

"Normally boys measure their penises with a twelve-inch ruler," I inform them. "I measure mine with a micrometer."

"Ball!"

Ignorance is bliss, so I keep rolling. "It's humiliating when I use a public toilet. The other men stand there, unzip their flies and this ruddy great thing plops out. I unzip my flies and stick my hand in and start to rummage around muttering, 'I know it's in here somewhere, I remember putting it away last time'."

Pinky and Perky are grinning, Gerta looks outraged, Brill has his head down, and Hazzard and Bligh are exchanging exasperated looks. Splendid.

"When I finally find it and pull it out and the other men do the usual of sizing up the opposition out of the corner of their eye," I continue, "they look at mine and a tiny smirk appears on their face. It's degrading and humiliating. I hate using public toilets."

"Yes, Ball, I'm sure this is very troubling," interjects Hazzard.

"No kidding!" I tell him. "It destroys your self-confidence having such a small penis. Still, look on the bright side, when I go to a nudist camp, at least I'll be let in at a reduced price."

"Now, what I wanted to talk about was – "

"No, seriously though, I'm quite happy with my penis – little things please little minds as they say. The best things come in small packages." I look directly at Hazzard, meet his exasperated gaze. "I call it 'The mighty midget'. What do you call yours?"

Hazzard has had enough of this, so he repeats his question.

"Seriously, how are you?"

Time to change tack. "Obviously, I'm pissed off," I tell him. "I'm an innocent, sane man, working hard to prove his innocence, and you are stopping all my letters, preventing me from getting the evidence I need to prove my innocence to the world!"

Hazzard chooses to ignore this and changes the subject. "Mr Bligh tells me you don't talk to him or the other nurses?"

"Of course I don't talk to him, he's absolutely repulsive." I glance over at Bligh, whose face is turning a troubling shade of puce. "Not only is he physically repulsive – he's fat and ugly – he's also mentally repulsive. He never talks in a normal tone of voice, is always shouting, and every second word is a swear word. I find it nauseating, he makes me feel sick." I look back at Hazzard. "I may be locked up in this hell hole, but I still have standards."

Hazzard has a sickly smile on his face, can sense this getting out of hand, but has no idea how to stop it. "Really, Ball, I'm sure it's not that bad?"

"Not only does his personality make me feel sick," I continue, "but his physical presence also makes me feel sick. He smells. Because he's fat he overheats and sweats. When the sweat dries it smells. This makes him smell excruciating because, not only does he have this smell, he also has the normal smell of the screws. The two combined are overwhelming. It's a wonder that the inmates don't throw up every time he walks by."

"I see, well I don't think – "

I'm not done yet, ignore Hazzard's protests. "Because he is so fat, I've nicknamed him The Fat Controller after the foreman in the kids TV programme Thomas The Tank Engine," I inform Hazzard. "Because the foreman is fat and is in control they nicknamed him The Fat Controller. As Bligh is fat and in control, I call him The Fat Controller."

Hazzard laughs uncomfortably. "Let's not get personal, now."

"Why not? Not only is Bligh a right dictator, he is also an evil bastard. He regularly punishes me for no good reason. He gave me a week's extra work just because I hadn't been on extra work for a long time," I protest. "A week's extra work! That means being on my hands and knees, scrubbing the floor all day long, for a week, then going to bed at the god almighty hour of seven o'clock."

"That doesn't sound right. I'm sure Mister Bligh wouldn't do that." Hazzard glances at Bligh for help, but Bligh is staring at me with a look of utter hatred, chewing furiously on his moustache.

I look at the others. Pinky and Perky are still grinning, Brill has his head down pretending he's not there, while Gerta is gazing at Bligh with a look that looks suspiciously like admiration, one vicious sadist to another. Time to finish up, deliver the coup de grace. "He really is a petty-minded bastard. I actually find it amazing that someone so physically big can be mentally so small, so very, very small."

I look to my right, a beatific smile on my face, see Bligh glaring at me with a look of pure hatred. I have no doubt that if he could, he would leap over the table and set about me, tearing me limb from limb.

Hazzard coughs, mops his brow. He is looking scared, is obviously concerned for my safety. He tries to lighten the mood, asks, "Are there any nurses you do like?"

"Well, Mr Brill is OK," I say, waving my hand in the direction of Mr Brill, who is sitting a couple of feet further down from Bligh. "At least he's got a sense of humour."

Brill looks up with a shy smile.

I smile back at him. "Mind you, if you look like that you have to have a sense of humour," I add. "Poor old Mr Brill. He should have encouraged his hair follicles to become best mates, that way they wouldn't have all fallen out."

Brill reflexively rubs his hand across his bald head.

"Look at that great bald dome," I continue. "He looks hideous with hair emanating from around the base of the dome and stretching down almost to his shoulders. And then there's that great bushy beard that occupies the bottom half of his face. It looks like he's got his head on upside down."

Brill actually laughs at that.

Pinky and Perky are still smirking, while Gerta is practising her glaring.

"Mind you he's very intelligent – he's got a high forehead, it goes right to the back of his neck." I'm warming to my task. "Did you know that he had a starring role in the Christmas panto?" I tell Hazzard. "He was the rear end of the pantomime horse. He was perfect for the role because his hairless, bald head meant he couldn't tickle the balls of the bloke playing the front end."

Brill laughs out loud, gets an admonishing look from Bligh, a 'don't humour him' glare.

"I don't know why he doesn't have a hair transplant," I say.

"If he had his pubic hairs transplanted to his head he would have a nice curly head of hair. Then, when a pretty girl strokes his hair it would give him a sexual thrill. It's the only hope he's got."

Hazzard attempts to stem the flow. "You seem very preoccupied with Mr Brill?"

"Well, the poor sod can never get married," I tell Hazzard. "If he looks like that now, imagine what he looks like first thing in the morning. If his wife woke in the morning to find such a vision confronting her she would think she was in bed with an alien and the shock would kill her."

Hazzard interrupts again. "Your hair's thinning," he tells me. "You'll soon be bald. Presumably this will mean that girls will find you repulsive?"

"Girls don't find me repulsive," I tell Hazzard. "I get on famously with girls, when I come into contact with them socially. But the only time I come into contact socially is when I am on holiday."

Hazzard scribbles something on his notepad.

"When I was nearly 17," I continue, "I had a holiday at Butlins Holiday Camp in Bognor Regis. There was a group of girls I got on well with and I ended up shagging one of them."

"That's just one incident," Hazzard points out.

"Also, when I was 21, I had a holiday in Tossa de Mar, Spain. At the end of the holiday, four different girls offered me their bodies. I declined because, by this time, I had made love twice, so I knew I didn't enjoy sex."

"I put it to you that this is all fantasy, you've never had sex," says Hazzard. "You're too weak and inadequate to get an erection."

Feeling affronted, I immediately respond. "That's rubbish! When I was sixteen, I had sex with my next-door neighbour. I'm sure she will be only too willing to confirm this in court. I'm sure the Butlin's girl will also give evidence if required."

Hazzard has a smirk on his face. "Fine. Tell me what a girl's clitoris looks like?"

"It's situated at the top of the vagina and looks like a tiny male penis," I inform him.

"You've seen this, have you?" snaps Hazzard.

"My probation officer lent me a book entitled, 'The A to Z of Sex'," I snap back, "and there was a diagram of a girl's vagina in it. I've never seen it in real life," I add.

"If you've had sex twice, how come you've never seen a girl's vagina?" charges Hazzard.

"The first time the girl was already in bed so I couldn't see through the bedding," I tell him. "The second time it was pitch black so I couldn't see anything."

Hazzard looks at me for a long time before responding. "A girl's clitoris doesn't look like you think," he tells me. "It's a small mound at the top of the vagina. Frank put that drawing in the book to establish whether or not you have had sex. We still don't know. We need proof you can make love to a woman. If we got a woman for you, would you have sexual intercourse with her?"

I find the turn in the conversation disconcerting. "I'll only make love to a girl I know and like and who knows and likes me," I tell him. This has gone on long enough with Hazzard in control. I decide to go on the offensive. "I'm not too inadequate to make love to a woman, but you are," I tell Hazzard. "You're a doctor, and it's every girl's dream to marry a doctor, but girls don't want to marry you because they hate and detest you, because you're so obviously weak and inadequate."

"You know nothing about me," Hazzard replies quickly, but I can see he is rattled. Seeing him on the defensive, I press home my advantage. "It's because you're weak and inadequate and can't have dominance over women that you have to have dominance over the patients. You rule here with a rod of iron and demand absolute obedience to try and make up for your lack of dominance over women."

"This case conference isn't about me, it's about you," protests Hazzard. "so if we can kindly return to – "

I lean forward in my chair, stare at Hazzard. "You're a gutless weakling. You're a poofter. I bet you prefer little boys to girls. I am young and pretty, you must fancy me. Go on, give us a kiss!" I purse my lips and make loud sloppy kissing noises. "Do you like my body? How about my legs?" I roll up my right trouser leg above the knee, wave my bare leg in the air. "Feast your eyes on that!" I tell him. "That must give you a sexual thrill."

Hazzard squirms uncomfortably in his seat, scribbles another note.

Pinky and Perky both have their hands to their faces, covering their laughter. Gerta looks most disapproving. In a sing-songy voice I add, "Who's got an erection then?"

"Mister Ball," says Hazzard in a serious voice. "Can we please maintain focus?"

"Yes, sir of course." I try to look contrite, but can't manage it. "No, seriously though, do you like them?" I waggle my leg at him again. "I'll admit they're a bit hairy, though not as hairy as hers." I wave a hand in Gerta's direction.

This goes down well. Gerta has finally cracked, and is laughing her head off, as are Pinky and Perky. Baldy Brill has a broad smile. Hazzard, however, looks sick and a bit guilty, while Captain Bligh is staring at me with a look of murder in his eyes.

"You're very cheeky today," Hazzard admonishes.

"I know I'm very cheeky, you don't have to tell me!" I laugh.

Hazzard tries to turn the focus back onto me. "Well if you're not intimidated by women, why didn't you ask any of the girls in your workplace out on a date?"

"Because I like to keep my work life and social life separate," I shoot back.

"Remind us of the jobs you had."

I sigh. This again. "I did mostly clerical work and driving jobs. My last regular job was as a chauffeur bearer at W.S. Bond's Funeral Directors in Shepherd's Bush. I didn't like that, it was a dead end job. But funeral parlours are friendly places - every body is welcome, and the clients are all happy, they never ask for a refund."

"Please try and remain serious, Ball."

"Of course. Let's see. Before the funeral directors, I had a job as a deep-sea diver but I left because I couldn't stand the pressure. Before that I had a job in an orange juice factory but I got fired because I couldn't concentrate. I also got fired from a calendar factory because I took a day off. But that's not to say I haven't had my share of responsibility. I once had a job with 500 people under me."

Hazzard scans his notes. "I don't recall that."

"I cut the grass at the cemetery."

Hazzard gives me a pained look. "I understand you were gainfully employed for nearly all your adult life. When did things go wrong? When did you become anti-establishment?"

I shrug. "I never was anti-establishment. I even voted Tory at the February '74 election. I only became a working-class dissenter after I'd experienced life in Rampton. Any society that maintains such a hell-hole as Rampton must be sick."

"I'm not sure that's a fair description of Rampton. We try to – "

I cut him off. "It's not only the regime in Rampton that proves this society is sick, there is also the fact that the people at the very top – the Prime Minister and Home Secretary – are evil criminals."

"What makes you say that?"

"Princess Anne must know it was a hoax, and it is inconceivable that she wouldn't have told her mother about it. In turn, the Queen would have had to tell the Prime Minister about it to make sure he was on board and wouldn't expose her and take steps to prosecute her. And the Prime Minister would have had to tell the Home Secretary. So it is obvious that, in this society, the people of highest authority are criminals, guilty of the serious crimes of kidnapping, threats to murder, torture, conspiracy to pervert the course of justice, etc. This proves that it is a sick society."

"All very interesting," says Hazzard with a fake smile, "but I think we could all do with a break. Coffee anyone? Brill, would you be so kind as to get us some drinks?"

While Brill scurries off to get coffees, I watch the others in the room.

Pinky and Perky are chatting happily together. As Hazzard didn't have the courtesy to introduce them, I can only speculate as to what their role might be. I study them further. They are both quite young – early twenties at most – with a fresh-faced, innocent look. They clearly haven't been corrupted by the system yet, so I conclude that they must be students or interns of some sort. I hope for their sakes that they get out before they are worn down by the daily grind of a place like Rampton.

Bligh and Gerta are also deep in conversation, with repeated surreptitious looks my way. Bligh is obviously telling her about me. Something about her look suggests that she is his superior, and that he is trying to impress her. Or maybe he just fancies her, with her hairy legs and hint of a moustache. Compared to Bligh, she is probably a catch. I look away quickly before my mind starts to imagine the two of them locked together in lust. There are some things that it is not good to even imagine.

That leaves Hazzard, the odd man out as usual. Hazzard appears to be busy reading my file, but it's an act, a front. There's nothing there he hasn't already read, that he doesn't know. In reality he's just trying to look busy, trying to disguise the fact that in a room full of people he is alone. No one looks at him. No one wants to talk to him. He is an inept outcast. Looking at his weak face I decide it is time to up the ante further.

Brill wanders back in with a tray of lukewarm coffees, has even brought one for me.

Hazzard sips his coffee, looks around. "Well then, if we're all ready…"

"I'm not."

Hazzard stares at me as though I've just taken a crap in the punch bowl. "Yes, very funny, Ball. Let's continue." He peers at his notes. They are his defence, his claim to superiority. He is the only one who has notes, has a file, and he wants to be sure everyone knows it. "Ball, you were explaining your theory that the kidnapping was a hoax, a reflection of…" he reads some more. "A sick society. Do you not think it is time to admit to what you did, to begin to move on?"

I stare back at Hazzard. "No. I don't. I think it's time for *you* to admit that the authorities are falsely and illegally detaining me because I am a very dangerous working-class dissenter and they don't want me to be able to express my dissenting philosophies."

"Philosophies," grins Hazzard. "That's rather a grand word."

"And yet it is the correct one," I tell him. "Britain isn't a fair democratic society as it professes to be, it is an upper-class dictatorship – every sphere of influence is in the hands of the upper class. They use their dominance to exploit the working class. For example, because they own and control all the big businesses, they can force the workers to work for low wages. By rights there should be a statutory minimum wage. This would prevent the worst cases of exploitation."

"How very socialist of you," he grins.

I ignore him. Having got my stage and my audience, I am determined to express my opinion. "It would also help prevent exploitation if a law were passed protecting the workers from discrimination and harassment and victimisation on the grounds of political beliefs, religious beliefs, age, disability, gender, marriage, race or sex." I tell him.

"Is that it?" He's clearly feeling piqued that none of the others are laughing with him. Pinky and Perky have lost their grins, Bligh and Gerta stare stony-faced at the wall opposite, while Brill has his head down.

"Something else I would like to see is a housing tribunal that a tenant can go to and give evidence in person if he considers he has been unfairly evicted or if he thinks his rent is too high," I tell them. "The complainant should have access to unconditional legal aid so that someone who is not very intelligent or not very articulate won't be put at a disadvantage."

This is not what Hazzard was expecting. "I see. Now back to – "

I ignore him, keep going. "Another thing is that the working class should have an equal right to a decent education. At the moment only a select few from the middle and upper classes go to university. I would like to see all the working class who are capable going to university. I am sure that at least half of working-class pupils are capable of going to university."

"Clearly we allow you too much thinking time, what?" He grins toward Bligh, who ignores him, continues to stare straight ahead.

"Mind you it may be difficult getting the Government to implement my policies given the state of the present-day politicians," I admit. "Nowadays, to succeed in politics it's often necessary to rise above your principles. 99% of politicians give the rest a bad name. Mind you, everybody has the right to be stupid. It's just that politicians abuse the privilege. Politicians and nappies have one thing in common. They should be changed regularly and for the same reason."

Hazzard looks exasperated. "The problem with you, Ball, is that you refuse to take anything seriously," he tells me.

"Au contraire," I reply. "I take everything seriously. Everything except you, that is, because you are a complete joke with your fifty pence haircut, your scruffy jacket and your gormless face."

I look around me to see how things are going. Gerta is looking bright and alert and laughing. She clearly prefers my insults to my political polemic. Pinky and Perky are obviously enjoying themselves, smiling broadly. I'll bet they didn't expect this much entertainment when they came here today. Baldy is also enjoying himself and smiling, though trying to hide it. Only Captain Bligh looks troubled, standing staring at me with a malevolent look on his face, his eyes boring into my head. I can feel the waves of hate washing over me.

Hazzard decides to try and restore some sanity to the proceedings. "Do you take illicit drugs?"

I shake my head. "No. I tried sniffing coke once but the ice cubes got stuck in my nose"

Brill stifles a giggle.

"Seriously," I continue, "I have never felt the need to take artificial stimulants. I didn't even smoke normal cigarettes or drink alcohol. Just going for a walk in the park or along a seaside prom gives me a high."

Hazzard looks disappointed. "You know," he tells me, "you're incredibly boring."

I lean forward in my seat. "Maybe I am, but that's because I am a great man. When you go into it, most great men turn out to be boring. I'm great because although I'm locked up and seemingly helpless, I can still get the authorities to implement my policies and change the world."

Hazzard frowns. "Why would you say that?"

"The authorities will have to implement my policies," I explain, "because, although they are torturing me to break me and make me recant my beliefs, they are saying that they are helping me. Therefore, they have to implement my policies to prove they are helping and not harming me. They desperately have to do this because if I were able to prove they were torturing me, there would be a public outcry and they would all be sacked, prosecuted, and sent to prison." I smile charmingly at Hazzard. "And you and Captain Halitosis over there – " I nod towards Bligh – "will be top of the list."

Hazzard has no answer to this so he decides to bring the proceedings to a halt. "I see, I see," he says, trying to sound like he has any clue what is happening. "Well I have no further questions. Do you have any questions you would like to ask?"

I tilt my head back, stare at the ceiling. "Why me?! God! Why me?!" I howl at the ceiling. Then I quickly look back at Hazzard. "That's it."

I stand quickly, head out the door. Another fascinating case conference is over. And the outcome? Bligh hates me more than ever, and Hazzard is more confused than ever. Mission accomplished.

Chapter 14

As I emerge from the room, I find Clive – or Evil C as he prefers – waiting for me.

"You were in there a long time," he informs me, "I was afraid they were putting the thumb screws on you." He glances around at the empty corridor. "Me and some of the boys," he glances at his imaginary gang, "was fixing to come in there and bust you out."

"Thanks C," I tell him. Friends come in all shapes and sizes and disguises, and Clive is definitely one of my friends in Rampton.

Clive falls in step beside me as I head for the rec room. "I don't trust that weaselly one," Clive tells me.

"You mean Hazzard?"

"Yeah. Keep an eye on him, I think he's a snitch for the feds." He grabs my arm. "If you have any trouble with him, let me know, and me and the boys will take care of him." He makes a gesture of slitting his throat. "Capiche?"

"Capiche."

"Good man. Catch you around."

And with that he sidles off.

I collapse into a chair and stare at the ceiling. Much as I enjoy my verbal jousts with Hazzard, I also find them exhausting. Combined with the medication they force on us, I find that I need more rest than my activity levels would suggest.

I struggle through the rest of the day, eat my meagre dinner, and am delighted to finally get back to my room having survived another day in the asylum still alive and without being kicked to death by the psychopathic screws.

I have just finished making my bed when the cell door opens and a young woman walks in. "Knock, knock," she coos.

I immediately recognise her as Dante's wife. I recognise her from her visits to see her husband on the admission ward. She is a vision of loveliness, with a cute pixie face, soft, shoulder-length shiny-brown hair, wide hazel-grey eyes and a pale, flawless complexion. Her slim figure is enhanced by an elegant skirt and a tight-fitting white blouse.

She's obviously not one for small talk. With a sweet smile in her voice she says, "I've heard you have certain powers?"

"Powers?" I mumble. Her perfume washes over me, driving me crazy. What the heck is happening?

"Powers with women? To, you know, give them certain gifts."

I have no idea what she is talking about, but she looks and smells so good that I just agree. "Yes, that's true," I admit.

She comes straight to the point. "Would you like to make love to me?"

Taken aback, I stutter, "We…….Well, ye……yes"

She walks past me to the bed, hurriedly takes off her clothes, lies down on top of the covers with her right leg bent at the knee, splayed open, the left jutting at an angle so that I can see the velvet mound between her thighs.

God! That's a beautiful sight!

"Come on then," she whispers. "We don't have much time."

I immediately rise to the occasion, whip off my pyjamas, and climb on top of her. She reaches up with both hands, cups my face and draws it down until our lips meet. We kiss passionately, a wet tonguey kiss.

As our kiss deepens, I slide my hand down her neck and body to her perfectly formed breasts. My hands cup and massage them, my fingers toying with her nipples, which instantly harden and stand to attention like firm jelly sweets.

Those glistening orbs look so enticing, I plunge my face into her cleavage and take a great wet mouthful of her succulent left breast while my cheek presses against the soft warm flesh of her right breast.

She moans softly as I continue my journey down her body to her thighs and the dark triangle of hair between them like a pointer to enticement. I part her lips with my fingers and massage her sensitive nerve bundle, then dip two fingers into her wetness, sliding deep into her warmth.

She groans, helpless with desire, and her hips arch against mine. I fit my hips to hers and thrust hard and deep into her. Her muscular tube begins to spasm, squeezing me. I come, my spine arching in a violent spasm, then breathless and drained, collapse face down on top of her.

Barely have I finished when she slides out from beneath me, starts getting dressed.

Within two minutes my erstwhile lover is fully clothed and heading out the door. "That's it?" I murmur. "Not even a goodbye?"

As the door closes I lie there and ruminate. What the hell was all that about? Why would she do that? Perhaps she saw me on the admission ward and fancied me? Ha! That's a laugh, I bet she's never even noticed me before. Or maybe it's a service she provides for all the patients? Impossible. I would have heard about it a long time ago.

Then it hits me. At our previous meeting Hazzard had said that I can turn women's bodies back, and they can look young and beautiful and live forever, with an IQ of 160 and a photographic memory. Somehow, Mrs Dante has heard about this and wants these perks. Why not? Providing such a service is certainly not something I would object to. It only takes a few minutes of my time and costs nothing.

I gaze at the ceiling thinking of the future that awaits me, thinking of all the beautiful women out there eager to avail themselves of my services. A smile crosses my face. I'm going to have a great time when I get out. Then reality hits. I've got no chance in here, they're stopping all my letters so I can't get the evidence to prove I'm innocent.

I've got to get out.

Is that madness? On one level it might seem to be so, but then

I consider – Hazzard himself is clearly so sure of my abilities that he persuaded Mrs Dante to have intercourse with me. If I did not have the power to turn her body back and enhance her IQ, the coupling would have been rape, to which Hazzard would have been an accessory. If charged and convicted of accessory to rape, Hazzard would be given a hefty prison sentence. There is no way he would have taken the chance of this happening.

Maybe it is all true? I vow to redouble my efforts to get out.

The following day, my thoughts are still in a mess as I sit in the day room. On the one hand I can still picture Mrs Dante in my room, still smell her intoxicating perfume on me as we made love. But at the same time her appearance in my room, her desire to have access to my powers, has highlighted exactly what I am missing by being locked up in here. If I were outside, and my powers were publicly known, I could have a woman like Mrs Dante – or better – every day. Casanova himself would be envious of my life.

It is in this state that I watch as the screws rush into the rec room to break up a fight. It's a normal state of affairs, something that happens several times a week over something as trivial as what TV show to watch.

However, on this occasion, one of the protagonists, the walking beanpole known as Rail, decides it would be a good idea to give some lip to the screws. In an instant the screws turn on him, allow the other inmate to scurry away, and lay into Rail with their fists and their boots. By the time they are done with him he is limp, bleeding, barely conscious. They drag him away, leaving a trail of blood along the corridor.

Pike spots me watching this in horror, marches up to me. "Ball! What are you looking at? Go get a mop and clean up that hallway!"

I am too tired to argue with Pike today, so I meekly do as he says, get a mop and start cleaning up the blood. It's a mess and takes a while, so I have only just finished when Rail reappears.

He looks a right state, his head bandaged, two black eyes, his lip split and still bleeding, and one arm in a sling.

Pike watches as he limps back into the rec room. "Oh dear, Mister Winters," he crows. "It looks like you tripped on your big, flat feet and fell over. Do be more careful next time."

I stare at Pike with hatred, and he looks over and sees me looking at him. "We can do the same to you," he says, with a malicious smile on his face.

For some reason I completely lose it. "Are you threatening me?" I demand. "Are you fucking threatening me?"

Pike stares at me for a moment, eyes wide, frozen with fear, before marching to the office. He's obviously going to tell Bligh.

I think fast. I could get into serious trouble here. I need to do something, and do it fast. I go to my locker and get out my newspaper, quickly take it back to my seat, start reading, pretending to be totally absorbed. Hopefully, if I act completely normally and pretend I can't remember what happened, Bligh will think I was talking subconsciously and won't punish me.

Sure enough, a couple of minutes later Bligh and Pike appear in the doorway. They stand there for a short while observing me while I pretend to be totally absorbed and not to have noticed.

After a moment they come over. Mr Bligh stands in front of me and says, "Alright?"

I jump, as if I didn't know he was there, look up and say, "Yes. Fine, thank you Mr Bligh."

Before he can say anything further I bury myself in the newspaper again.

The two of them shake their heads, then walk away. I got away with it this time, but I can't afford any more screw-ups like that if I am to get out of Rampton. I decide there and then to put my escape plan into operation without any further delay.

Chapter 15

Another month, another meeting with Hazzard. Despite the frustrations I experience every time I meet with Hazzard, I nonetheless understand that he is my conduit to the world. Like it or not, if I am to achieve any of my goals, I am going to have to deal with my annoying RMO.

As I settle in my seat, under Bligh's watchful eye, Hazzard scans my file in a self-important manner. We all know that he already knows every word in there – he wrote most of them – and he also knows exactly what he wants to discuss on any given day, but scanning through my file emphasises that he is in control. He has the file. He has the power to keep me waiting.

In order to not let him have his own way, I spend the time studying my hand as though I have just discovered something fascinating on it. He glances at me once or twice, and eventually can't resist the bait.

"Ball. What are you looking at?"

I jump like a teenager caught in the act of masturbating, sit on my hand.

"What's going on with your hand?"

"Nothing. Nothing at all."

Hazzard gives a deep sigh of frustration, gives Bligh the signal to go check out my hands. As Bligh approaches, I hold my hands out to him as though getting ready for a manicure. "Lovely, aren't they?"

Bligh peers at my hands, gives a weary shake of his head. "Nothing." He plods back to his station by the wall.

Hazzard looks puzzled. "Well why… Oh never mind. Now

listen here, Ball. Bligh informs me that you want to transfer out of Rampton to Broadmoor?"

I nod eagerly. "Yes, indeed, sir."

Hazzard frowns. "Aren't you happy here?"

That is probably the most stupid question I have ever been asked, but I don't rise to the bait. Instead I try to give a reasoned reply. "It would be a lot better for me there," I explain. "This is a hospital for sub-normals, whereas the patients in Broadmoor are intelligent, so there would be more people for me to talk to and make friends with, ipso facto I would be happier."

Hazzard shrugs. "I suppose that might be true."

"Also," I continue, "it is a lot closer to my hometown so I would feel more at home and it would be easier for my mother to visit. Oh, and last but not least, I would get a new RMO there, who might be inclined to allow my letters to go out."

At the mention of the last topic, Hazzard gives his weary little smile. "Now, now, Ball. We've been through this over and over again. I don't block your letters. If you don't get the responses you're looking for, maybe you should consider sharpening up your letter writing skills."

Normally this condescending lie would be a red rag to a bull for me, given the overwhelming body of evidence I have proving that Hazzard has spent years blocking my letters, but today I am determined to remain calm. "I assumed that you would obstruct me," I tell him, "so I am hereby giving you fair warning that if you do not allow me to transfer to Broadmoor, I will go on a thirty day hunger strike in order to prove to the world how unhappy I am here, and how desperate I am to get to Broadmoor."

Hazzard chuckles in his annoying way. "Really, Ball? You expect me to believe that you would really go on hunger strike? You've spent most of your time here complaining that we don't give you enough food."

"In which case," I reply quickly, "it won't be much of a loss for me to give it up all together, will it?"

This gives Hazzard pause for thought. He turns to Bligh. "Is he serious, Bligh?"

Bligh gives a wiggle of his luxuriant moustache. "It is my experience that when Ball says he intends to do something, he usually sticks to it."

Hazzard looks exasperated. "You really mean to go through with this?"

"Do you really intend to keep blocking my letters?"

Hazzard frowns. "I don't know where you get this absurd idea from."

"I recently sent two letters," I explain, "to the 'Sun' and 'Daily Mirror', giving brief details of how everything concerning my case was a hoax and how I am an innocent, sane man. I haven't heard a reply from either."

"Maybe they have better things to do than answer your letters?"

"Oh, I'm sure they would reply," I tell him. "In the one to the 'Sun' I pointed out that a reporter from the 'Sun' was at the scene when the hoax kidnapping was taking place, and even intervened. Therefore the reporter must know it was a hoax, and so the editor must know also."

Hazzard starts to interrupt, but I keep going.

"In the one to the 'Mirror', I pointed out to them that they had published details of my Local Wag exploits, so they must be in with Frank and must know it was a hoax. In each letter I threaten to sue the newspaper if they don't get me out, so I'm pretty certain they would respond – if they had ever received the letters."

Hazzard shakes his head. "Doesn't ring any bells for me. Bligh?"

Bligh shakes his head. "Nothing for me."

"In that case," I inform them, "I will go on hunger strike, and stay on hunger strike until you allow me to send the letters."

Hazzard leans forward, smiles. "In which case, I will prescribe another round of ECT to offset your provocative and obstructive behaviour."

Stalemate.

And so I begin my hunger strike.

Although this makes my life markedly more unpleasant because I no longer have even the small pleasure of a meal three times a day I am determined to see it through.

Bligh, of course, does everything he can to break my will by regularly appearing in front of me with tasty treats which he then devours – a sugary donut, a chicken sandwich, a choc ice – but I manage to stay strong, do not allow them the satisfaction of besting me.

After a couple of days they start forcing Complan down me and weighing me every day. They can't make me eat their meals, but they will do whatever it takes to stop me actually dying on them. That would make the hospital look bad.

I decide that I can't simply wait for Hazzard and Bligh to cave in due to my hunger strike, so in the meantime, I launch another strategy. As Hazzard is stopping all of my letters to the press and politicians from getting out, and thus preventing me from getting the evidence to prove that I am a sane, innocent man, I launch an appeal and explain to the appeal court how I have been trying to get the evidence for an appeal but that Hazzard has been preventing me from doing this by stopping my letters. This will create documentary evidence of my predicament. It's a process that unfolds step by painful step.

Firstly, I have to get the application form. I, therefore, write to the appeal court requesting the form. The court refers me back to the hospital social worker, tells me I have to get the paperwork from him.

Predictably, the hospital social worker refuses to give me the form.

I, therefore, write again to the appeal court, telling them this. They tell me to persevere with the social worker.

So once again I write to the social worker telling him what the appeal court has said. He still refuses to supply the form.

Once again I write to the appeal court. They reiterate that I have to get the form from the social worker.

I vow not to give up, and continue my hunger strike in the meantime.

The first few days are the worst as my stomach shrinks and I learn to endure the gnawing hunger pains. It seems that wherever I go during meal times the smell of food wafts over to me, so even without Bligh eating his treats in front of me I am haunted by food. But early in the second week, a strange thing happens. I wake up, and am not immediately consumed by thoughts of food. In fact, I feel great. Bligh chooses that day to come by with a thick, greasy sausage in his hand, but as he bites into it and the grease runs down his chin, I breeze past him with a smile on my face. "Morning, Captain."

He swallows hard, can't contain his look of disappointment at my casual reaction. My triumph is short-lived however. As I make my way to the day room, Hazzard is waiting for me. "Ah, there you are Ball," he says breezily. "Time for your first round of ECT."

Once again I am faced with the horrors of ECT, the memory loss, the risk of being reduced to a drooling vegetable.

"Who's that sitting in the corner?"

"Oh him? That's Ball. But these days we just call him Broccoli."

I'd like to say 'no thanks doctor', but that is out of the question. Hazzard has made the decision, and Bligh has a smile on his face as he leads me to the treatment room. Two burly orderlies follow us, but they are not needed this time. I learned previously that it is no good fighting, that it's going to happen, with or without my approval, so I might as well be cooperative and get it over with.

I lie down on the bed, docile as a lamb, and Bligh straps my ankles, wrist, and forehead.

After a short wait, Hazzard trots in, all false bonhomie. "Good morning everyone. Lovely day today, isn't it?"

I can't turn my head to look at him but reply anyway. "You wouldn't think it was such a lovely day if you were the one strapped to this bed," I tell him.

Hazzard just laughs, leans in to peer at my face. "Ball. Ever the joker."

"I'm not joking," I tell him. "I'd happily trade places. You can be the one getting a hundred volts fizzed through his brain, the one to suffer the confusion, the memory loss, and I'll be the one trotting round in the white coat playing God."

Hazzard has clearly had enough of our little chat, so he ignores me, nods to Bligh to prep me for the ECT.

Bligh makes strong eye contact with me as he sticks the pads to my forehead, clamps the bite protector between my teeth. He wants me to know how much he enjoys this.

I meet his gaze, don't flinch, don't look away. He is not going to see my fear.

"There," says Hazzard, "it looks like we are all ready." He nods to the anaesthetist. "Let's put him under."

And that's the last thing I remember for a while…

Two days' later, Bligh once again summons me. I fear it's for another round of ECT, but instead, he leads me into Hazzard's office.

Hazzard's usually cheerful demeanour seems to have deserted him. He wastes no time getting to the point. "Mister Bligh tells me that you are still on this ridiculous hunger strike?"

"For some reason," I tell him, "the ECT hasn't changed my mind, or made me forget what I am doing and why."

"And you are bound and determined to continue with it?"

I nod. "To the bitter end."

"I was afraid you might say that." Hazzard gives a deep sigh, looks down at his papers. I realise that Bligh is glaring at him, and Hazzard is avoiding looking at Bligh. Have they had a falling out? A disagreement?

"I've been reviewing your file," Hazzard tells me. "And it does appear that some of your letters may have been held up or lost due to an administrative error."

It takes me a moment to process what he is saying. "So my letters…"

"Any future letters that you write will make it out of here and reach their intended recipients."

I can't keep the smile off my face. Hazzard has caved in. I've won. I turn to Bligh. "What's for dinner tonight?"

Bligh glares back at me. "A shit sandwich for you if you don't wipe that silly smile off your face."

"Mister Bligh?"

Bligh gives Hazzard a false smile, returns to me. "I believe it is Spaghetti Bolognese, Mister Ball."

I stand up. "Sounds wonderful. See you at dinner!"

A couple of days later the 'Sun' and 'Mirror' publish articles about me.

Chapter 16

Although I have, hopefully, succeeded in getting my letters out, it has become clear to me that I am going to need a much more drastic strategy if I am ever going to succeed in getting transferred to Broadmoor.

Hazzard is still adamant that I will never be transferred to Broadmoor and keeps on trying to persuade me to take part in the various therapies offered in Rampton. Unless I can give him a compelling reason to get rid of me, I'll be stuck in Rampton forever. I rack my brains and eventually come up with a cunning plan. I call it "Operation Spook Hazzard", and it involves Timothy as an unwitting accomplice.

The plan is simplicity itself. If I can convince Hazzard that I am going to murder him, he will get rid of me to save his life. Obviously I can't directly threaten to murder Hazzard, so I have a chat with Timothy. After his regular beatings, Timothy has become a full-time snitch, willing to shop anyone if it means he gets less abuse in return. As I sit down next to him, I know that anything I tell him will soon find its way back to Bligh, and then on to Hazzard.

"I've had enough!" I announce dramatically as I slump into the chair next to Timothy.

He gives me a startled look, instinctively looks around.

I continue as though he weren't there. "Hazzard has refused my transfer request – again! So I've decided that I'm going to kill him."

This is grist to the mill for Timothy. He leans in closer. "Really kill him, or are you just saying that?"

I look at him properly for the first time. "Really kill him," I confirm. "I've got it all worked out." I lean in conspiratorially. "When I've murdered him they'll put me on trial. That will generate news worldwide, give me the chance to finally explain how the kidnapping was all a hoax, and how Hazzard, on orders from above, has been stopping my letters to prevent me from proving it." I glance around, rub my hands together as though warming to my task. Tim gulps, hardly able to believe the nugget that has just landed in his lap.

"As the highest in authority in the land has been involved in all of this," I continue, "it will cause a public scandal and the British Establishment will be subjected to such international opprobrium that the trial judge will have to treat me leniently." I smile. "I'll probably only get six years for manslaughter – I mean, you couldn't really blame me for killing Hazzard, could you?"

"No indeed," confirms Tim.

"With a third off for good behaviour, I would only serve four years, which would mean that I would be released immediately as I've already served more than four years in Rampton." I finish with a triumphant look on my face. "Brilliant, right?"

Tim nods eagerly.

I clutch his arm, whisper. "Of course, you can't tell anyone any of this, it would ruin everything if word got to Hazzard." I look around furtively. "I can trust you, can't I?"

Tim nods vigorously. "My lips are sealed," he whispers, then does that stupid thing of pretending to zip and lock his lips and throw the key away.

"How will you eat or drink?" I ask him, then jump up and stride away while he tries to figure out the conundrum I left him with.

It doesn't take long to see a result. The next day I am called in for an unscheduled interview with Hazzard. He looks scruffier than usual, with bags under his eyes. Bligh is on duty as usual, but even he looks twitchier than normal.

"How are you?" begins Hazzard. He is fiddling with his pen, looks ready to bolt at any moment.

"I'm fine," I snap back. "How about you? You look tired?"

Hazzard ignores my question. "Are you getting on with everyone?"

I nod vigorously, the very picture of bonhomie. "Everyone apart from the screws of course," I tell him. "But they are all psychopaths, nobody gets on with them." I glance at Bligh, who is furiously chewing on his moustache. "I expect they even hate themselves."

"You hate the screws?" wonders Hazzard.

"Of course I do."

"Do you think of doing them harm?"

I give a beatific smile. "Of course not. I'm a very easy going, unaggressive person."

Hazzard ponders this for a moment, finally asks the question this has been leading up to. "What about me. Have you ever had any thoughts of harming me?"

"No!" I try to sound shocked that he would suggest such a thing.

"You must hate me because I won't transfer you to Broadmoor," persists Hazzard.

"Yes. But I would never do physical harm to you."

Hazzard seems unconvinced. "You don't want to kill me?"

"Of course not."

"Hmmm." Hazzard studies me for a minute. "You seem a bit restless, I'm going to increase your medication."

"Oh, thank you doctor," I reply sarcastically.

Hazzard is already writing the prescription. "That will be all."

I leave, trying to keep the smile from my face.

The seed has been sown. Time for phase two – find a way to convince Hazzard that I have an appropriate weapon.

Later that afternoon I get my radio out of my locker and sit in a chair in the TV room. I choose my seat carefully, making sure that I am as far away from the day room screw as possible, but where he can still clearly see me.

I begin to act suspiciously, looking at the plastic disc on the bottom of the radio, which could potentially be broken and used as a sharp weapon.

In due course, the screw comes over to see what I am doing, whereupon I pretend that I have just noticed the day room screw looking at me, pretend to panic, and rush over to put the radio back in my locker.

Surprise, surprise, that evening the screws inspect all the patients' radios. When they come to mine, they unscrew the plastic disc and confiscate it.

I scowl at Bligh. "Why are you doing that?"

"Orders," he says cryptically.

"Whose orders? Dr Hazzard's?"

"Just orders," he tells me.

The seed is burrowing deeper. Time to water it…

The screw stares at me. "What do you mean you want a wet razor? You never use a wet razor."

I stroke my cheeks seductively. "I've decided I want a closer shave. All the ads on the telly suggest that I'll have more success with women if I have a better shave."

"You never meet any women," points out the screw.

"I just want to be ready when I do," I snap back.

The screw shakes his head. "Sorry, no can do."

"What! Other people get to use a wet razor. Why not me? I know how to use one. It's not like I'm going to cut my throat with it."

"Nope!"

"That's discrimination!"

We're making such a racket that two other screws come and join in the argument, surround me, shouting, cursing, swearing and threatening.

Eventually I give up, look disappointed as I walk away.

Following this performance, it's time for another chat with Timothy. He is sitting at the back of the rec room picking his nose and staring listlessly at the TV.

I drop into the seat next to him. "Can you believe that?" I say. "I wanted a wet razor, and the screws refused to give me one."

Timothy nods sympathetically. "I heard the row."

"The thing is," I continue. "I really need one." I grab his arm, as though I've just had a great idea. "Say, you couldn't get one for me, could you?"

Timothy once more gives me his startled deer look, but then rallies around. "I could try."

"Good man. And keep this to ourselves?"

"Of course."

"Cross your heart? Hope to die?"

Tim nods.

"Excellent." I skip off as though I am the happiest man in the world.

The following morning, Hazzard approaches me in the day room, two screws hovering close behind him.

"I hear you had an argument with the staff the other day, what was that all about?"

"They wouldn't let me have a wet shave."

"Why did you want a wet shave?"

"Because it is a closer shave compared to an electric shaver, and will make me more alluring to women." I give him a big smile.

Hazzard frowns. "You don't see any women, Ball, and anyway you look alright to me. You don't need a wet shave."

"I beg to differ."

Hazzard can barely conceal his nervousness, hopping from foot to foot. "When I last saw you, you said you had no thoughts of harming anybody. Is that still the case?"

"Of course. Why would that have changed?" I am perched on the front of the chair, my back straight, leaning towards Hazzard with my right hand closed to give the impression that I am concealing something – maybe a razor blade? My face looks tense, as though I am about to leap forward and slash Hazzard's throat.

Hazzard keeps looking at my hand then looking around at the screws with a scared look on his face, his hands noticeably shaking. I am obviously having the desired effect on him.

Hazzard peers at me. "What's in your hand?"

I try to look guilty. "Nothing." I squeeze my hand closed even tighter, the knuckles white with the effort.

"Open it!" demands Bligh.

I swiftly pass my right hand over my left hand, which is on my left thigh, close my left hand and open my right hand, then hold it aloft.

Hazzard's eye twitches. "What's in your left hand?"

"Nothing," I tell him again.

Once again Bligh jumps in. "Open it."

I repeat the hand switching manoeuvre, like a street trickster performing the three cups ruse.

Hazzard looks ever more agitated. "Stand up!" he barks.

I scowl. "I beg your pardon?"

"Stand up!" shout all the screws in unison.

I shrug my shoulders and slowly rise. "If you insist."

The screws close in, make a close inspection of the lower half of my body, the floor below it. "Nothing."

Hazzard's eye is in full twitch mode. "Get out!" he shouts.

I slowly turn, says a polite, "Thank you, sir," and stroll out.

That went well.

I have been having intermittent toothache for a few days, so the screws reluctantly agree to take me to the dentist. This involves walking along the main hospital corridor, past the hospital's Reception area.

As the screws escort me along the corridor, Hazzard comes through the door at the end of the corridor, head down, muttering to himself. Suddenly he looks up, spots me, panics. For a moment he freezes, then, in complete disarray, does a swift U-turn and, fumbling with his keys, unlocks the door and swiftly exits.

"Nice to see you, Doctor Hazzard," I call after him. I turn to the guards, a big smile on my face. "He was in a funny mood today, wasn't he?"

I am barely back from the dentist when Bligh comes to see me. "Hazzard's office, now!" he shouts.

My face is still half numb, so I struggle to speak coherently. "Waffor? Not on the schedule."

"Now!" insists Bligh.

I stand up, obediently follow him into Hazzard's office. When I sit down, Bligh takes up station behind me, instead of taking his usual place leaning on the wall.

"I'll get right to the point," says Hazzard. "The clinical team and I have had a discussion, and we have come to the conclusion that your mental condition has improved to such an extent that you are now ready to go to Broadmoor."

I feel my heart skip a beat. I've done it!

"That will be all."

A short while later, on the 4th December, I am transferred to Broadmoor.

Chapter 17

There are 20 patients in the admissions ward at Broadmoor, a mixture of mentally ill and psychopaths, old and young. Unlike Rampton there are no subnormals, which is a relief. Hopefully I'll find more people with whom I can have an intelligent conversation.

The staff – 5 on the ward per shift – wear screws' uniforms. Some of them are kind and compassionate, some detached and cold, some cruel and domineering.

I wander round, find the usual facilities – a kitchen, dining room, bathroom, toilet, washroom, office, medicine room and day room with a 22inch colour TV, radio and a half size snooker table.

A couple of hours after I arrive on the admission ward I am interviewed by Dr McGrath, who is the superintendent of Broadmoor and who will be my RMO while I am on the admission ward.

"Hello, Ian, I'm Dr McGrath." He is better dressed than Hazzard, more composed, less nervous.

"Yes, I know, I remember you from Brixton, you were the second opinion doctor for my committal."

McGrath smiles. "That's right, I'm glad you remember me. How much do you remember about the index offence. How do you feel about it now? Do you feel any regret or remorse?"

Wow, I think, no preamble, no foreplay, straight to it. "Why should I feel regret or remorse," I tell him, "I've done nothing wrong, I've committed no crime. I'm not guilty of attempted murder because the gunpowder had been taken out of the bullets, and I'm not guilty of attempting to kidnap Princess Anne because that wasn't Princess Anne in the car."

McGrath looks vaguely uneasy. "Now Ian – " he begins, but I cut him off.

"You must know that, you must know it was a hoax? When you interviewed me in Brixton I thought it was 1974 and not 1975, so I must have been living one year behind everybody else, and the amount of contact Frank and his associates would have had to have with me to maintain the time deception proves that it would have been impossible for me to plan and execute a real kidnap attempt."

McGrath scowls. "I can assure you that nobody told me it was a hoax, and as far as I am concerned it took place in 1974."

This isn't going well. "You're lying!" I protest. "You must know it was a hoax?"

McGrath changes tack. "What about Dr Hazzard, does he know it was a hoax?"

"Of course he does. We discussed it many times."

McGrath frowns. "Hang on a minute." He picks up the phone and rings Hazzard.

I sit patiently while he explains what I just said, listens intensely for a short while, then puts the phone down. "Dr Hazzard says he doesn't know what you are talking about."

I sigh. "Well, he would, wouldn't he?" I tell him. "He has lied and obstructed me for years. That's why I have spent so much time trying to get transferred here."

McGrath scans my folder. "Do you find your present medication is helping you?"

"How can it help me when there's nothing wrong with me?"

My answer seems to surprise him. "I think I'll review your medication," he tells me. "Thank you, that will be all."

A couple of hours later the charge nurse informs me that Dr McGrath has changed my medication to Modecate. I'm not happy. If anything, Modecate is even worse than my present medication. Side effects include blurred vision, constipation, dizziness, drowsiness, decreased sweating, weight gain and erectile dysfunction. Granted, the last one isn't a major problem in Broadmoor, but I'm not keen on the others.

Accordingly, when the screws show up the next day to try and inject me with the Modecate, I resist.

Things quickly become heated, and before I know it a dozen burly screws wrestle me to the floor, pick me up and carry me to a side room, dump me face down on a bed, yank my trousers and pants down, and ram a huge needle up my arse.

As the screws shuffle out, one of them turns and grins at me. "Welcome to Broadmoor."

Despite this rude introduction, the regime at Broadmoor is generally more easy going than Rampton. The screws treat the patients like something resembling human beings, there is no scrubbing or decking and, for most people, there is no ward work at all. However, I once more find myself in conflict with the RMOs, and once again I discover that they are stopping my letters.

A typical conversation goes like this.

"You're blocking my letters again."

Dr McGrath folds his hands in front of his chest.

"This is to protect you, Ian, it's in your best interest."

"Why?'

"Because if we allowed your letters to go out, you would get adverse publicity in the newspapers. This would cause you distress, and ultimately mean you would spend longer in Broadmoor."

I shake my head. "You're wrong. If I can get my letters out I will be able to get the evidence to prove that this was all a hoax. I will then be released so, overall, it would be a lot less stressful."

"Sorry, Ian. We've made our decision."

Despite this, I continue to write letters relevant to the hoax, in the hope that some might get out, while at the same time continuing to write to both the appeal court, and now the social worker at Broadmoor, in an attempt to finally get the appeal form.

Finally, after nine months, I succeed, and am able to appeal against my conviction and sentence. Obviously, the appeal is turned down. But I have achieved my objective – I have documentary proof that Hazzard and now McGrath are stopping my letters and preventing me from getting the evidence to prove that I am a sane, innocent man.

At the same time, I continue to work on my autobiography. Initially, I see this as a backup, something to use if I don't manage to prove my innocence by sending letters, but as I lie on my bed at night I realise how important it will be. My biography will be the first opportunity for people to hear my side of the story, to counter the lies that Frank and the media have spread over the years, and to let the people who witnessed the incident at the time hear the other side of the story. There must have been a lot of ordinary members of the public in The Mall who witnessed the hoax, and for me to have been convicted, Frank would have had to persuade these people that I didn't know it was a hoax, and therefore that I must have thought that I had live bullets in my gun, and that I had actually shot people. I would therefore have been guilty of the very serious offences of attempted murder and attempted kidnapping and should be locked up, hoax or no hoax.

If I could publish my autobiography, however, I could show that I knew all along that it was a hoax, and the members of the public would see that they had been deceived, and that an innocent sane man had been falsely incarcerated and should be released immediately.

It is not easy to write, however, as I am in a constant battle with the side-effects of the various psychotropic drugs such as Modecate, Depixol and Haloperidol that I am forced to take. Focusing, remembering, writing, how can one do these things when suffering from fever, blurred vision, restlessness, muscle spasms, headaches, shakes, constipation, lethargy, drowsiness and a befogged brain? In truth, I feel that I am being subjected to a regime of drug torture in an effort to break me and force me to recant my beliefs. In addition, the doctors enjoy administering ECT, which further compromises my memory.

Nonetheless, I continue my battle to get my letters out to MPs, solicitors, barristers, The Criminal Cases Review Commission, newspapers, TV stations, book publishers, working-class unions, Amnesty International, The National Council For Civil Liberties and other civil liberty organisations. Clearly some of my letters escape RMO McGrath's net, as I receive occasional responses, but even though these remain overwhelmingly negative, trivialising or even ridiculing my premise, I am undeterred, and continue my letter writing.

In addition I place adverts in domestic and foreign, local and national, newspapers to find people who knew of my Local Wag identity, knew that I was living one year behind everybody else, and knew I had ESP, all of which are key planks in my quest to prove my innocence.

At the same time I launch various types of legal action in the High Court and the European Court of Human Rights. In the High Court I launch prosecutions for Conspiracy to Pervert the Course of Justice, False and Illegal Imprisonment, Kidnap, and Torture, while in the E.C.H.R. I launch an application under Article 5(4) to force the British Government to change the law to give the Mental Health Review Tribunals the power to order the release of the patient rather than just recommending their discharge to the Secretary of State, and an application under Articles 9(1), 10(1) and 14, which deal with freedom of speech. The aim is to establish that I am a political prisoner who is having his freedom of expression illegally curtailed by the Government.

Finally, I send letters to left-wing Labour MPs and solicitors who I think might be sympathetic to my cause, explaining that

I am an innocent sane man, and requesting that they help me to prove it and thereby effect my release. Predictably, the letters are returned by my RMO with a note saying he can't send the letters because the adverse publicity I would receive would cause me distress.

This is a serious blow, as the letters go right back to the beginning, explaining how I first met Frank when I was sixteen, in a car park in my home town of Uxbridge. Frank was a police officer on duty in the car park who thought I was acting suspiciously and decided to question me.

As I wasn't doing anything wrong, I refused to answer Frank's questions, but after the encounter Frank made enquiries and found out that I was a pupil at Greenway Secondary Modern School in Uxbridge, which he visited to get some biographical details on me.

His investigations at my school led him to discover that I was considered to be very intelligent and was the premier prefect. Frank thought that someone with these qualities would make a good police officer, however, when he approached me with the suggestion that I join the Force, I declined. Nonetheless, we became friends and continued to associate with each other, and often indulged in practical jokes.

Three years later, a practical joke involving the high street butcher went massively wrong and caused the town centre to become gridlocked. The traffic jam was reported in the local newspaper, 'The Middlesex Advertiser', which detailed all of the various practical jokes I had played on the pupils and teachers at school and on the general public in and around Uxbridge. The article covered the whole of the front page and a double inside page, and gave me the nickname, 'The Local Wag'.

I hated all the public attention I received as a result of the publicity, and so I dissociated myself from family and friends and fled to London where I rented a room under an assumed name and got a job in a local office.

It wasn't long before Frank discovered my whereabouts, however, and continued to force his attentions on me, setting up practical jokes. These jokes were subsequently reported in 'The Daily Mirror'.

In 1974, and growing increasingly fed up with Frank molesting me, I decided to go to court and get a restraining order to prevent Frank from coming anywhere near me. As I didn't have enough money to pay for the court action, I racked my brain in an effort to find a way of making the money. Eventually I came up with a cunning plan…

If I were to make out that I was going to commit a spectacular crime that would receive international publicity, Frank would secretly make sure I wasn't successful. He would do it secretly, however, because he would think that I was serious and would normally end up being arrested, prosecuted and sent to prison.

As Frank wouldn't want me to go to prison, he would let me think that everything was going according to plan, while at the same time secretly making sure that any props were neutralised (for example, by taking the gunpowder out of any bullets). This would make sure that no members of the public would come to any harm.

Certain that Frank would intervene appropriately, I pressed ahead with my plan. Firstly, I had to come up with a suitable 'crime'. After reading, in a book, a story about a hoax involving the Royal Family, I recalled that, four years ago, I had jokingly told an old work colleague, Mr Thorpe, that I was going to kidnap Princess Anne and demand a huge ransom. Mr Thorpe was an obsequious individual with a surfeit of dandruff, who had taken me seriously and had informed Frank of what I had said. Mr Thorpe then told me what he had done, presumably, to prevent me from carrying out the crime. This was it, my very own "perfect crime". It was time to put it into motion.

Chapter 18

Firstly, I had to surreptitiously let Frank know that I was going to commit the 'crime' by making use of my previous association with Mr Thorpe.

One day, while talking to Mr Thorpe it became clear that he had intimate knowledge of my bank account. On questioning, it transpired that someone had stolen a letter containing my bank statement from the table in the reception area of my rooming house, where all the tenants' letters were placed for collection, and passed it on to Mr Thorpe.

From this, I knew that if I left letters relevant to the hoax on the table they would be stolen and passed on to Mr Thorpe, who would, in turn, pass them on to Frank, thus alerting him to my intentions.

First, I ordered a biography of Princess Anne from the public library. When the postcard came telling me that the book was ready for collection, I left it on the table and it was, in due course, stolen.

I had told Mr Thorpe I was going to get the guns from Spain, and so wrote to several travel agents asking them to provide details of flights to Madrid. When I received the replies, I duly left them on the table to be stolen.

Next, I wrote to several estate agents requesting details of secluded houses for rent near Princess Anne's home in Sandhurst. When I received the replies, I left the letters on the table to be stolen. Thus Frank knew where the hideout was going to be.

Confident that Frank would now be fully alerted to my plan, I continued to make more solid preparations. I went to Madrid and bought the guns, then once they were home I put them in a cash box and put it in the safe of my branch of Barclays Bank. A month later I took one out and tested it, and confirmed that Frank had indeed taken the gunpowder out of the bullets.

Next, I rented a house near Princess Anne's house in Sandhurst, then rang the Press Office at Buckingham Palace and asked for details of Princess Anne's public engagements for the next couple of weeks. I was told she would be attending a function for the Riding for the Disabled charity at Sudbury House in the City of London the following Wednesday.

That was to be my D Day, and here I crave your indulgence. The book opened with an account of the kidnapping – the official version, as told from my perspective. What I am now about to detail is the real version, the hoax version, the version that explains how it actually happened, and reveals my innocence…

On Wednesday, I drove to Sudbury House, waited until Princess Anne left, then followed her car. As we rounded Trafalgar Square, the cars from the road on the left (Whitehall) hurtled towards me at great speed. To avoid a collision I was forced to apply the brakes and swerve to the right, temporarily losing sight of the royal car and allowing Frank to substitute a dummy car.

Once I had extricated myself from the traffic jam and caught up with the royal car I noticed that the position of its occupants had been reversed – whereas previously Princess Anne was sitting on the left with Captain Marks Philips on her right, now the man was sitting on the left, with the girl to his right. This was quite clearly a test of Frank's – if I hadn't noticed it I wouldn't have known that the hoax was in play.

I continued along The Mall, overtook the dummy royal car, brought it to a stop, immediately went to the girl's door, opened it and started talking to her.

Now, if it had been a real kidnap attempt, this would have been a crazy thing to do because Princess Anne's bodyguard would have simply walked up behind me and blown my brains out. If it had been a real royal car, a real kidnapping attempt, the first thing I would have done is go to the bodyguard's door, open it, and neutralise him.

However, this was not real, it was a hoax, and the man acting as the bodyguard knew it, because when I looked up after talking to the girl for a minute or so, the spoof bodyguard was just standing there looking at me. I pointed my gun at the 'bodyguard' and fired. This didn't have much effect so I pointed the gun at the girl and told him, "Drop your gun or I'll shoot the Princess."

The 'bodyguard' pretended to shit himself, and immediately dropped his gun on the floor. Now, a real police officer wouldn't have shit himself – they're made of sterner stuff – and he certainly wouldn't have parted with his gun so easily. However, by now it was clear that we were just play acting, so I pretended to forget all about the 'bodyguard' and went back to talking to the girl.

Now, again, if this had been real, this would have been a crazy thing to do because the bodyguard would have just picked up his gun, walked up behind me and blown my brains out. From there the spoof kidnap continued to unfold as described in the opening paragraph, with the key difference that no real bullets were fired, and no one was actually injured.

The other key issue that I explained in my letters to the MPs and solicitors, was why Frank didn't get me out of hospital when I wrote to him in December 1974.

On my arrival at Brixton Prison, after my trial at the Old Bailey, I was taken to the hospital wing and put in a cell. As soon as I entered the cell, I had a quick look around and checked to make sure there were no cameras, and once I had ascertained that there were none, I reverted to my usual juvenile self and started clowning and cavorting around.

After mucking about for around five minutes, I made a more detailed inspection of my cell, and found a small patch on the wall which had obviously just been re-plastered and re-painted. I surmised that this could be where Frank had placed a microphone to listen to me.

I continued my inspection, but when I looked up into the lampshade I was horrified to see a camera lens. Why on earth would anyone want to put a camera there, I thought? You can't see anything, the lampshade blots out 99% of the room, you would only be able to see a tiny spot directly underneath the lampshade. But that could have been enough. Frank would have seen me cavorting around. "Shit! You idiot, Ball!"

Deflated and subdued, I lay down on the bed, on my side, eyes closed.

A short while later, the cell door opened and a male voice said, "Are you coming?"

I immediately recognised the voice as Frank's, and pretended to be asleep.

"If you don't come now, it'll be out of my hands," added Frank.

I started to snore.

Frank gave a deep sigh, gently closed the cell door behind him.

Now you may be wondering why I didn't go with Frank? After all, that was it, my golden opportunity to get out, to avoid prison before it was all too late. The reason, quite simply, was that if I had done so at that point, it would have made the whole endeavour pointless.

The whole idea of staging the hoax was to get publicity so that I could publish my autobiography and get money for the restraining order and to buy a house for my future wife and kids to live in. It was important to me that my son was brought up in a healthy environment and didn't suffer the same fate as me – I had been brought up in a sub-standard council flat with terrible rising damp. Indeed, the damp had risen so far that it had even begun to fall. This moisture had damaged my lungs to such an extent that while the other boys could use the long course for the school cross country runs, this was beyond my capabilities. The first time I had tried it, it nearly killed me. As a result, the gym master allowed me to use the much shorter cross- country course in the future.

Although I would love to have taken Frank up on his offer of freedom, I was aware at the time that the newspapers couldn't print very much about my case whilst it was sub-judice, so I had to wait until after the trial before revealing it was a hoax in order to get the maximum publicity. Tempting as it was to leave with Frank and avoid the consequences that awaited me, I was determined to see it through.

I was proven right in the end as my life story was published in the 'Sunday People', for which my mother and sister were each paid £4,000 for their contributions, a not inconsiderable sum in those days.

As I lay on my bed listening to Frank's footsteps echo down the empty corridor, I wondered who Frank was referring to when he said it would be out of his hands?

It could be just a detective inspector in the Metropolitan Police, or, given the sensitive nature of the case, it could have been taken right to the very top and could be in the hands of the Prime Minister. If it were the former, I had some hope. If it were the latter, I had no hope, for they would keep me locked up in a special hospital for the rest of my life. As events have proved, the authorities were indeed determined to lock me up for the long haul.

Chapter 19

Soon after arriving in Broadmoor, I make an application to the European Court of Human Rights under Article 5(4). Article 5(4) states that people detained by the State should have their case examined, periodically, by a fair, impartial tribunal to see if their detention is still justified. I explain to the Court that, as my crime involved the daughter of the Head of State, in my case, the present Mental Health Review Tribunals were not fair and impartial as they could not discharge me, they could only recommend to the Secretary of State that I be released. I thus suggest to the Court that the tribunal should be headed by a judge who had the power to actually order my release.

While I wait for the response from the ECHR, I have my second case conference with the RMO, the Charge Nurse, the Psychologist, the Social Worker and the head of the Assessment Centre. It is a stormy affair, as I am in no mood to be conciliatory, and thus complain loudly about the side effects of the drugs and about the RMO's continued refusal to let my letters go out.

During the case conference, I repeat what I said at the Rampton case conference about the defects in the education system, and how that hindered people such as myself, who were denied the opportunity of a decent education.

The RMO seems sceptical, to say the least.

I point out again that if they had a decent education, half of the working-class pupils would be going to university, to which he replies that this is ridiculous, because most working-class children are far too stupid to go to university. He blatantly says that I am mad for suggesting such a thing!

My own experience is very informative in this regard. I failed the 11+ and went to a secondary modern school. At the time, people like me were seen by the authorities as worthless failures on whom it was not worth spending any time, money or effort – we were virtually written off. At school we had to endure dilapidated infrastructure, useless teachers and substandard teaching aids. You were lucky to get one text book for each subject you were taking, and even that had been handed down from pupil to pupil so many times that it was battered and dog-eared, with the cover and pages missing.

Our science lessons took place in a dilapidated Nissen hut with a leaky roof, situated at the far end of the school grounds, across a muddy field from the main building. Most of the time the teacher didn't even bother to turn up, and when he did he would just tell stories about his private life which, while entertaining, didn't impart any knowledge of the relevant subject. Laboratory equipment consisted of just three Bunsen burners and a pipette for thirty-six pupils.

It was under such conditions that we were taught GCE Science 'O' level, and not surprisingly, most pupils failed. I managed to pass because I worked hard, studying the decrepit course textbook, books I found at the local library, and old exam papers I got from the examination board.

I worked hard at all my subjects and, against all the odds, got six 'O' levels, which was the highest number in the entire history of the school. As there weren't the facilities to take 'A' levels at the school, I had to take a job at EMI, in Hayes, as an apprentice engineer, but in the evening I attended Southall Tech and got the ONC in Electrical Engineering, with credits in 4 out of the 5 subjects, which was considered the equivalent to 2 'A' levels.

If I'd had a decent education, I would have probably got 9 or 10 'O' levels and 2 'A Levels and gone on to university (at the time, you only needed two 'A' Levels for a place at university). If that had been the case, the course of my life could have been completely different.

In the end I believe that I have been proven right in my assertion that with the right opportunities, working-class children can succeed in the education system, and I believe that my written communications with Tony Blair almost certainly gave rise to his famous mantra 'Education, Education, Education' and led to his radical transformation of the education system.

Nonetheless, at the end of my case conference it is decided that I be transferred to Cornwall Ward and that I should work in the Radio Shop.

Cornwall Ward wears a familiar look to the various wards I saw in Rampton. It has a kitchen and a dining room, washrooms and toilets, food lockers and a day room, a full size snooker table and a table tennis table.

There are 40 patients on the ward of all races, creeds and colours. Half sleep in side rooms on the ward, the rest sleep in the dormitory two flights up on ward three, which is where I am installed.

At lunchtime, I get my food and sit down opposite a large patient in a stained T-shirt. I immediately regret my decision to sit with him, but decide it would be too rude or provocative to simply get up and leave, so I quietly begin eating.

My table mate shovels some food in his mouth with his fingers, looks up at me. "Who the hell are you? I haven't seen you before."

"I'm Ball," I inform him, "I've just arrived."

"Thought so." He shovels more food in, then holds out a meaty paw, covered in food, for a hand shake. "Bentley."

Be polite, I tell myself, don't provoke anyone until you know the lie of the land. I carefully shake his hand, then wipe my hand on my trousers.

Bentley makes firm eye contact with me, then slowly removes his glass eye, rolls it around on his plate and starts flicking it at the peas as if playing a childhood game of marbles. "Marbles!" He says gleefully, waiting for my reaction.

What can I say? "Yes, marbles," I echo.

Bentley picks his eye up, pops it in his mouth to clean it.

Suddenly he starts choking, coughing, spits bits of food and his glass eye out. The eye flies over my head. I try to catch it, but it slips through my fingers and rolls away under a chair.

Bentley is still coughing and spluttering, so I retrieve his eye from under the chair, clammy, messy and wet, return it to him.

Bentley gives it a quick wipe on his shirt and pops it back into place, then resumes shovelling his food down.

There's a screw standing in the dining room doorway watching all of this. He shakes his head. "You messy bastard," he says.

Bentley just grins and keeps on eating.

Not surprisingly, I've lost my appetite. I return my tray, wander into the day room. Another patient nods to me. He's skinny, with long, scraggly hair down over his collar. He gestures for me to sit beside him. "I see you've met Bentley," he says by way of introduction. "That's his party trick with newcomers – see if they'll pick that disgusting eye up."

"And I fell for it?"

"I wouldn't call it that. If you hadn't, he would have thrown his food tray at you."

"Interesting character," I observe.

"Oh, you don't know the half of it." He leans in closer. "You should hear how he got in here." He laughs in anticipation. "He'd already done time for armed robbery, so the local police had an eye on him. Anyway, one day he's feeling a bit hungry, and is out of money, so he picks up an old toy gun he has that looks just like the real thing, puts a pillowcase over his head, and robs the local supermarket of a pint of milk, a loaf of bread, a half a pound of butter and a jar of strawberry jam.

"However, Bentley being Bentley, he has somehow forgotten that the supermarket is opposite the local police station, and a copper who is looking out of the window sees our friend fleeing the scene. Now although our man has his face covered, he is wearing his trademark purple, fluorescent shirt with a giant multicoloured serpent printed on the back, so the copper knows right away who it is.

"So the police pile into their squad car, race round to Bentley's house, and arrive while he is in the process of making a jam sandwich with the aforementioned stolen comestibles. Brilliant, eh?"

"We all have our moments," I reply ruefully.

Chapter 20

As I settle into Broadmoor, the horrors of Rampton begin to fade, and I can once more turn my attention to my campaigns These are all areas where I feel my campaigning skills might be able to affect a change in society, namely:

(1) Getting a public enquiry into Rampton, and extracting a measure of revenge for the beating I received on the admission ward. This will also benefit the current inmates who still suffer under the brutal regime there.

(2) Getting the 1959 Mental Health Act changed. This would directly benefit me as it would mean I could write to MPs, solicitors, and others of influence, thus advancing my campaigns, and would also permit me to have a tribunal every year, which would have the power to discharge me.

(3) Getting a reduction in the dominance of large companies by the upper class.

This is something that directly affected me when I was younger and applied to numerous companies for a job, but failed to be hired by any of them. At the time I was unable to understand the reason for this, however, when I was in Rampton, Hazzard one day let it slip that the managing directors of the various companies I had applied to were all upper class, so Frank had found it easy to persuade them not to hire a working-class dissenter such as myself, telling them that they would obviously not want to be the ones to provide me with the money to finance my rebellious activities. And in the end, it was my inability to get a decent job that forced me to embark on the risky hoax escapade.

(4) Getting the law changed so that the police no longer made the decision as to whether or not a suspect should be charged and brought before a court.

Again, this was something that I had personally experienced. It involved the setting up of a stationery supply business and the sending of a £4.50 cash on delivery parcel, actions that were considered to be illegal by a certain police officer. When he arrested me, I explained to the officer that what I had done wasn't illegal, and showed him two letters from different solicitors stating that fact.

At the court hearing I drew the magistrate's attention to the existence of the letters and he asked to see them. However, the police officer denied all knowledge of the letters, and there was nothing I could do to provide them, as the officer had made sure I was remanded in custody by refusing bail, thus preventing me from retrieving the letters from my property at the police station and showing them to the magistrate. As a result I was kept in prison, on remand, for six weeks, before being forced to plead guilty and given a small fine.

(5) Getting the authorities to reform the education system so that working-class pupils could get a decent education.

The main weapon in my armoury is my written communications with newly elected Prime Ministers, explaining the improvements I thought should be made to society. I reasoned that the incoming PM would have had no choice but to carry out some of these improvements because, if my prolific letter writing had succeeded in making the affair public, the Prime Minister would have been better able to calm the resulting storm by saying he had been helping me build up my self-confidence by taking my suggested improvements seriously and implementing some of them.

Meanwhile, I am slowly getting used to my new environment at Broadmoor. One of the biggest changes is sleeping in a dormitory. At Rampton I had got used to having my own room, but that is not the case at Broadmoor, so at the end of my first day on Cornwall Ward I follow the crowd, traipse up the stairs to the top ward, where the dormitory is located.

I am allocated a bed next to the toilet. Not ideal, but making the best of a bad deal, I make my bed, climb in, and start to read my book – 'The Innocents'.

As I try to concentrate, a stream of patients go in, one at a time, to urinate.

I know what they are doing, because the toilet door does not close completely, always remaining slightly ajar.

Then two patients go into the toilet together, and through the crack I see that they are sharing a joint. Things are clearly different in Broadmoor than Rampton.

When they have finished, three other patients go in, one clutching a large bottle of scotch.

I wonder if I should ask, "Is this a private party or can anyone join in?" as I watch them imbibing, but my attention is drawn by two effeminate-looking patients opposite me, bickering and bitching like an old married couple. They are obviously husband and wife, and soon stop arguing and become all lovey-dovey.

The husband starts giving his wife big wet sloppy kisses. I can't see what he sees in her, I think she's an ugly cow, but I suppose there's no accounting for taste.

The husband then takes off his wife's, and his own pyjama tops.

The wife has large, milky white breasts, most likely the side effects of the medication "she" has been taking, which the husband begins to mould and massage. He then bends down and takes one then the other into his mouth, swapping between them as if he can't decide which he likes best.

Watching them is disgusting and I try to avert my eyes, but it's like driving past a horrific car crash, you try not to look but you just can't help yourself.

Things are starting to heat up as they both remove their pyjama bottoms and the wife takes hold of her husband's erect instrument, pulls it towards her mouth, and begins to play the skin flute.

I look round at the other residents of the dormitory to see how they are reacting, find that they are not taking a blind bit of notice. It seems that this is a normal everyday occurrence.

The horror show continues, and I find myself unable to look away as the husband grabs hold of his wife and manoeuvres her so that she is kneeling with her backside facing him. He quickly mounts her and begins pounding himself into her.

I think I'm going to be sick, but human nature being what it is, cannot look away, have to watch it through to the bitter end.

Fortunately that arrives quickly, as his head jerks back and he cries out before withdrawing and collapsing in a heap on the bed beside her.

They both lie there groaning for a moment, then, finally, the noise subsides.

Thank God for that, I think.

Now that the connubial unpleasantness is over, I can go back to my book.

Now, let's see, where was I? Oh yes, "Little Charlotte took her mother's hand and looked up at her with an innocent smile…"

On the 22nd May 1979, a show airs on Yorkshire Television entitled, 'Rampton, The Secret Hospital'. The programme exposes the ill treatment of the patients by the screws, and is considered to have been made to such a high standard that it is awarded an International Emmy.

The exposure leads to a Public Enquiry, which is conducted by Sir John Boynton, which results in the prosecution for assault of dozens of screws, including the three who beat me up on my arrival.

Delighted that I have finally got a public enquiry and that it has led to criminal prosecutions, I write to the Chief Constable of Nottinghamshire offering to give evidence at the forthcoming court hearings. However, the Chief Constable refuses to deal with me and, instead, writes to Broadmoor's superintendent, who communicates with my RMO and thus on to me.

The summary of what the RMO tells me is that the Chief Constable doesn't want to have anything to do with me, yet another case of the closing of ranks between the upper-class Chief Constable, the upper-class doctors, and the upper-class Ministers.

Further good news comes when I discover that as well as the Public Enquiry, it appears that we are also going to get a new Mental Health Act, one of the key recommendations of the Enquiry.

When campaigning to get a new Act, I had, on numerous occasions, given explicit details of what I would like included. One such proposal is the absolute right of a patient to be able to write to MPs and solicitors. If this is included, I will finally be able to write to these two groups of people, which will make a tremendous difference to my other campaigns.

Another track I have been pursuing is through the European Court of Human Rights, who inform me that the Court has asked the Government if it wishes to submit written observations of admissibility in my case.

Shortly thereafter, I receive another letter from the Court stating that the Government is willing to waive admissibility of the Application, and a few months later, yet another letter saying that the Application is admissible. I feel like I am finally getting somewhere – however, things soon turn complicated when I receive copies of the Court's judgement.

On inspection, I discover that my Application has been successful, and the Court is asking for my proposals for a friendly settlement. I write back saying that I don't want any damages, to which the Court writes asking why I don't want damages.

In my reply, I explain that I didn't take the legal action for financial gain, I took it because I thought it was wrong and unfair to patients that when they apply to the tribunal, the tribunal can't discharge them. If I took any money, it would make the whole affair feel grubby and dirty. Clearly the court and I have a different perspective on these matters!

Chapter 21

My mind continues to return to what RMO Hazzard said about being one year behind everybody else when I was outside, decide to try and figure out how they could have changed the year without me noticing. I come to the conclusion that they did it on the 1st January 1972, eight months before my 25th birthday, the day I returned from my holiday in Morocco.

The night before, the hotel had held a six-course banquet with unlimited free champagne. I over-imbibed and, as a result, was paralytic – I remember it well because, on the day of departure, the tour guide was incensed that I kept the whole party waiting for an hour while I was being sick and defecating. Not my finest hour…

I also remember that I thought I was going to die and that all I was interested in was making peace with my maker – thus the actual day, date, or year were of no concern to me whatsoever. If that were when the switch happened, I begin to wonder why I didn't discover the deception after I had got home and sobered up?

I conclude that it was probably because I didn't have a diary or anything else to remind me of the date, and I didn't have anyone who could have informed me of the deception, because I had no friends as I spent all my time working.

I decide that it is time for me to start searching for evidence to support this.

My quest to establish whether or not I was living one year behind begins by writing to the Newspaper Library in Colindale and requesting photocopies of the front pages of all the national newspapers for the editions published on 21st and 22nd of March 1974, the days when the hoax was front-page news.

I am excited when the papers arrive, pore over them for anything that might support my theory. Everything appears to be in order, until I notice the reports are exactly the same across all the newspapers, whereas normally, one would expect to see great differences when reporting a fast-moving, complicated event that had only just happened, where the journalists and editors were rushing to make their paper's deadline.

As I look more closely, I also notice that the bullet hole in the rear windscreen of the royal car is obviously one of those joke bullet holes that had been stuck on the windscreen.

However, though these observations are interesting, they are not conclusive. I, therefore, try another method, obtaining a copy of 'The Whitaker's Almanac' in order to look at the date for the appropriate Wednesday. If I was living one year behind, the date of the Wednesday would be the 19th and not the 20th, as I believe, but when I check, everything is OK. But again, this is inconclusive, because I could also have been living one day behind everybody else, in which case the date would be the same – the 20th.

As I lie in bed at night, trying to ignore the shenanigans taking place in the nearby bed, something else occurs to me. I remember that when I went to get my Private Pilot's Licence, the office clerk insisted on filling out the application form himself – in fact he was very aggressive about it, began shouting at me. I refused to be intimidated and insisted on filling out the form myself before handing it back to the clerk for him to fill out his part.

I was hoping that he had put the date before handing it over because, if he had, he would have then had to cross it out. Hopefully, when I receive a copy of the licence, I will be able to study the date and ascertain what it was and if it was the same as my date.

Unfortunately, when a copy of the licence arrives, it shows that the clerk had not got as far as filling in the date, so this method also proves to be inconclusive.

Ultimately, after rejecting a number of options, I come up with a fool proof way of proving the time difference. In the second week of August 1972 I went on holiday to the Isle of Wight. I remember it was rainy on the first and last days, but for the rest of the week the weather was excellent, with the middle three days being over thirty degrees.

All I have to do is get the weather forecast for the second week in August for the years 1972 and 1973 and see which one fits. The problem is, how can I get the weather forecast? If I get the data from the Met Office or buy a book, Frank will be able to falsify it. I rack my brains further in an effort to find a solution to the problem, grateful for something to distract me from the Mister and Mrs show.

In the meantime, the 1982 Mental Health (Amendment) Act is published, and I obtain a copy from Her Majesty's Stationery Office. The Amendment Act gives details of the changes to the 1959 Act that will be included in the new 1983 Mental Health Act. I study the document carefully, and find that everything I said should be included in the new 1983 Act has been included. For example:

The Mental Health Review Tribunals are now headed by a judge, and the tribunals now have the power to order the discharge of a patient.

A patient can now apply for a tribunal every year instead of every two years.

Patients have an absolute right to write to MPs and solicitors.

A special health authority known as The Mental Health Act Commission (MHAC) is also to be set up to protect the rights of the patients, including overruling the RMO when he stops a patient's letters.

Excited, I show my copy of the 1982 Mental Health

(Amendment) Act to the RMO, point out that when the 1983 Act comes into force I will have an absolute right to write to MPs, so he might as well let me write to them now. To my amazement the RMO agrees.

Finally free to fully unleash my campaigns, I prepare to send letters to all Labour MPs.

First, I buy a portable typewriter.

Then I type a six-page A4 Hoax Explanation document, and send it to a printer to have 100 copies printed.

Once I receive the printed document, I type four covering letters and send them, together with the Hoax Explanation, to four individual Labour MPs. The covering letter runs to three A4 pages and explains how I am being forcibly and illegally detained by the Government because I am a very dangerous working-class dissenter.

I point out that if the affair were made public, it would cause a constitutional crisis and would result in the fall of the Conservative Government. Labour would then be elected to be the ruling party.

Each day I send out a further batch of letters until I have written to over 300 MPs. Over the next few weeks I receive about 100 replies, most of which just say that they have sent a copy of the letter to the Home Secretary for his comments. Good luck with that!

As the above exercise seems to be proving fruitless, I change tack, write to 400 solicitors, sending them the Hoax Explanation and a covering letter asking them to prove that I am an innocent, sane man, and to take the appropriate legal action to get me out. Once they have done this, I suggest that they take out a private prosecution against the Prime Minister for conspiracy to pervert the course of justice and false and illegal imprisonment. Although I receive many sympathetic replies over the coming months, none propose legal action.

I refuse to give in, so next I write to the heads of government of twenty major countries. I receive several interesting replies, for example, Mr Muldown, the Prime Minister of New Zealand, says he has sent my letter and his reply to the British High Commission, but once again, none of them take on my case.

Finally, in late 1983, I have my first new tribunal as set up under the 1983 Act. As soon as I walk into the tribunal room I can see by the look on the panel members' faces that they have already made up their minds and, in my case, it is not going to be a favourable outcome. However, we all have to go through the motions.

The judge begins by asking me a number of questions, then he hands me over to the tribunal psychiatrist. When he has finished his probing, it is the turn of the layman to ask questions. Next, the judge asks my RMO to say his piece, followed by the hospital social worker.

Finally, the judge asks my solicitor for his legal arguments. Up until now, the whole process has been mind-numbingly tedious, but now the place comes to life, with the judge and the solicitor in their element, arguing points of law, quoting previous cases, sparring back and forth. Then just like that, the performance is over, and everybody files out.

After ten minutes in a cold corridor sitting in a blue plastic chair, everybody files back in and the judge announces that, surprise, surprise, my application hasn't been successful.

Oh well, I guess that's it for another year…

My letter writing continues, this time targeting Amnesty International, the International Commission of Jurists, the Howard League for Penal Reform, the International Court of Justice, The British Journal of psychiatry and the International Committee of the Red Cross, none of which bears fruit.

In a separate matter, I also write to the Press Council complaining about an article in the 'Sunday People', which lambasts me, making me out to be a common vicious criminal.

I explain to the Press Council that the incident was a hoax, that I am an innocent, sane man, and point out that the 'Sunday People' must know all of this because they are the sister paper of the 'Daily Mirror', who know it was a hoax, and would surely have told the 'Sunday People'?

The Press Council gives me short shrift.

I return the favour by lambasting the Press Council, saying that although they are supposed to keep the newspapers in check by investigating complaints, in fact they do the opposite, covering up the newspapers' transgressions and letting them off the hook.

I hear nothing further.

As we move into 1985 I write to the following organisations:

(1) The Appeal Court seeking permission to appeal to the House of Lords.

Permission is refused.

(2) The MHRT asking them to make sure that all the members of my forthcoming tribunal are of masculine gender. I explain that as my crime involved a member of the Royal Family, and women are much more likely to be ardent royalists, they are less likely to be able to take an objective view of my case.

(3) 'The Middlesex Advertiser'. This is the local newspaper for my home town of Uxbridge. I insert an advert appealing for members of the general public who can remember me as 'The Local Wag' to contact me.

(4) The Queen. I say that I am in no doubt that she is under the misconception that she is helping me but, in fact, my confinement is doing me a great deal of harm.

To refresh her memory, I enclose a copy of the Hoax Explanation. I suggest that now that she knows the truth, she should get me out. I receive no reply.

(5) The Paddington Mercury. This is the local newspaper for

the area in London where I used to live and work. I send them a letter requesting that they print an advert asking Mr Thorpe to contact me. This letter is blocked by my RMO.

(6) A detective agency. I negotiate to hire a private detective to find Frank. The detective says it will cost £500 and the deal is set. But then I find out that the private eye is an ex-copper, and don't trust him to be impartial, so the deal is off.

(7) Other organisations. E.g. The Haldane Society, The Royal College of Psychiatrists, The World Psychiatric Association, The British Medical Journal, The United Nations Human Rights Commission, World Medicine, Justice and the Helsinki Declaration of Human Rights.

At this time I receive a letter from a division of Thames TV saying that they understand my position and would like to make a documentary about my case. I send them the Hoax Explanation and other relevant details, but never hear back from them, which is disappointing to say the least.

Chapter 22

Although I preferred having my own private room, sleeping in a dorm room does at least provide some entertainment, not least because we have a resident prankster, known to everyone as Ernie because of his uncanny resemblance to Ernie Wise.

I am assigned the bed next to Ernie, but rather than making me a regular target for his jokes, he sees me as something between an accomplice and a receptive audience, and as long as I laugh at his pranks and don't ever grass him up, my bed remains a prank free zone.

Ernie's pranks are definitely of the old school type – the first one I see him pull is to slip a bar of "joke shop" soap into another patient's shaving kit, then wink at me to ensure that I remain silent.

Come bedtime, the unfortunate victim heads into the bathroom to get washed up, and shortly thereafter reappears with a black face, hollering loud enough to wake the dead.

The screws come hammering in, thinking someone is being murdered, then stop and collapse in fits of laughter when they see what the commotion is about.

Another favourite trick of Ernie's is the fake poo, which appears at regular intervals in patients' beds, making them think they've soiled the bed in the night. It also shows up in the shower, the day room, even the canteen, leading me to think that Ernie must have a whole box of them in his locker.

My letter writing is taking up more and more time, so I change my place of work from the Radio Shop to the Mini Hanger because the hours are shorter, allowing me more time to pursue my campaigns. There are lots of differences between the two places.

The Radio Shop was much smaller than the Mini Hanger, with only five patients. There were also three patients in the adjoining Print Shop, and two in the hospital magazine's editorial office down the end. In the Radio Shop I had helped fix TVs, radios, headphones, electric kettles, toasters, and so on, and the occupational therapist in charge of the shop had tried to get me to take the City and Guilds in Electrical Engineering, but as I already had the higher qualification, the Ordinary National Certificate, I declined.

While the patients in the Radio Shop are among the most intelligent in the hospital, the Mini Hanger's 40 patients are the least intelligent – there are, however, ten female patients in the Mini Hanger. Together with the male patients they make cane baskets, trays, stools, rugs, bunny rabbits, etc.

With the female patients come female screws, including Cynthia, a beautiful blonde screw who sits next to me and chats happily to me. Like just about every male in the place I fancy Cynthia, and her face and figure fill my fantasies, however, I assume that she is probably a lesbian, as are most of the female screws.

With more free time, I up my letter writing. I am frustrated by the refusal of my RMO to allow the letter to the Paddington Mercury to go out, so I write to the RMO and inform him that I am going to complain to the Mental Health Act Commission about his refusal. To my delight, the Commission finds in my favour and the RMO inserts the advert.

I also get back issues of the Illustrated London News for the whole of 1974 and the first three months of 1975 so that I can closely examine the page containing the report of the hoax.

I subject these to a forensic level of examination, and notice that the colours on these pages are sharper than those on the other pages, which are a bit faded. Also, the staples holding the pages together are brand new on the edition containing the report, while on the other editions, the staples are tarnished.

The staff all know of my campaigns and protestations of innocence, so I discuss these findings with the Charge, who is both more intelligent and more sympathetic than most of the others, but while he agrees with me, he points out that it doesn't prove that the incident took place in 1975 and not 1974. I sigh in frustration. He is right.

In addition, I write to the members of the House of Lords who were in the House from 1968 to 1974, explaining my situation and asking them if they remember reading about my Local Wag exploits in the 'Daily Mirror', but again, get no fruitful responses.

Widening my search, I write to the Cyprus Tourist Office asking them for all the literature they have about the country. I do this because I visited there in 1973, so I want to study the literature to see if I can find anything that would prove that I was living one year behind everybody else, but like so much else, this proves to be a dead end.

As I lie in my dormitory at night, thinking of Cynthia and trying to ignore the cavortings of the 'couple', my mind constantly turns over the events around the kidnapping hoax, searching for something, anything, that will support my belief that I was living a year behind. As I do so, my mind turns again to something that Dr Scott in Brixton asked me when he was assessing my mental condition for my plea of guilty but insane. "Have you ever had any prophetic dreams," he wondered.

After much thought I told him that I had only ever had one, and that was when I was on holiday in Morocco in 1971. I had dreamt that I was driving in the Rif mountains. It was pitch black, and I found myself driving round and round in small circles, unable to find the road off the mountain.

When I went to the Rif mountains the next day, what I had dreamt came true.

I was mystified and could offer no explanation as to what had gone on, but Dr Scott told me that it had all been set up by Frank as a test, which I had passed with flying colours.

At the time I couldn't understand what Frank was testing me for, but since Hazzard had told me about my ESP abilities, I realised that Frank was testing to see if I could tell which direction to go in by just using my senses, without using any external clues.

If that assumption was correct, Frank had failed miserably, because I simply used plain logic to find my way out. I knew that when a car was travelling along the road the pressure on the stones forces them to the side of the road. Therefore, to find the right road off the mountain, all I had to do was pick the one of the two roads where all the stones had been forced to the side, as this would be the genuine road, not the dummy road.

However, to help me better understand the affair, I got all the relevant information from the Moroccan Tourist Information Office, including information about the Rif mountains. I also wrote to the RAC in Morocco to get information regarding my International Driving Licence, to Hertz to get information about the car I had rented, plus a variety of maps of the terrain in the area of the Rif mountains.

I also finally realize that the way to get absolute proof of the correct date, which I could show to everyone, would be to get the bank statements relating to two accounts I had when I was living in London from 1968 to 1974. I therefore write to the Midland Bank, Queensway, and the National Westminster Bank, Westbourne Grove, asking them to supply me with statements for the accounts I held at the banks. I do receive a reply from both banks, but both of them say that the requested items have been destroyed as they only keep such records for twelve years.

I write again to National Westminster pointing out that, although they would normally have destroyed the records after twelve years, in my case they would have had to keep them for longer than twelve years, as they would have known the records would be the subject of future legal proceedings. I tell them that, if they don't hand over the records, I will apply to the High Court for an injunction forcing them to release them.

Predictably, they refuse, and I therefore apply for the injunction, however, I have to abandon the proceedings before they have run their full course due to technical reasons.

Another possibility occurs to me. When I was on holiday on the Costa Brava, in Spain, I was annoyed that the Sunday papers weren't available until the following day, Monday. So, after obtaining my Private Pilot's Licence, I decided to fly the papers there in a light aircraft and get them there on the same day, Sunday, thus cornering the market.

The only glitch was that I didn't have a plane, so I went to Barclays Bank in Hayes, where I had an account, and asked for an £800 loan to buy a Jodel Ambassador light aircraft, but was turned down because I didn't have sufficient collateral.

However, according to Hazzard, I was living one year behind everybody else at the time, so I write to the bank requesting the records for the failed transaction.

They reply saying the records have been destroyed.

Another dead end.

When I was living in Uxbridge I used to go to the library every Saturday afternoon and, whilst there, used to interact with the librarians. They were all aware of my Local Wag identity, so I write to Uxbridge Library asking any librarians who were working at the library between the years 1966 – 1969 and who were aware of my Local Wag identity to contact me. However, when they reply, it is only to inform me that none of the relevant librarians are still working at the library.

Around this time I am kicked out of the Mini Hanger, now called the Activity Centre, because I am considered to be too intelligent for the type of work they do. Instead I wind up in Handicrafts. It is a large hut with 20 patients where I weave cane seats for antique chairs. Very intellectually stimulating.

In handicrafts I find myself sitting next to my dorm mate, Ernie. He gives me a wink, whispers, "I've got a new trick I read about. Be awake around midnight, you'll like it."

"Any hints?" I wonder.

"The couple," he says. "They've got it coming."

Ernie, like me and many others in the dorm, is fed up with the couple rutting every night – if they are his target, I'll make myself stay awake to watch.

That night, the couple perform their usual nightly copulation, then collapse against each other and fall into a deep, snoring sleep.

I glance over at Ernie.

He points at his watch, whispers, "a few more minutes. I want them good and asleep."

I lie back on my bed, gaze at the ceiling, wait. As I do so, I think of what I can do next in my efforts to prove my innocence, come up with a couple of ideas for the morning.

The sound of shuffling feet alerts me – Ernie taps my shoulder. "Show time."

I watch as he disappears into the bathroom, hear the sound of running water. He emerges a moment later with a bucket, tiptoes to the couple's bed.

He's obviously told several people about tonight's show, as I can see various other people sitting up on their beds to watch.

Ernie reaches the couple's bed, gazes down at them for a moment, then lifts a free arm from one of them and gently drops it into the bucket.

I instantly know what he is up to – putting someone's arm in warm water when they are asleep triggers the bladder to vacate itself.

Sure enough, within a few seconds, the victim wakes up, gives a squawk of horror, dashes for the bathroom.

This wakes his wife, who also sits up, looks down at the bed in disgust, then yells, "you wet the bed!"

Cue widespread laughter from the audience.

Chapter 23

As a result of my late night cogitations, I decide that it would be a good idea if I were to take steps to jog the memories of the readers of the 'Middlesex Advertiser' and 'Daily Mirror' who had read about the 'Local Wag' jokes, by relating the most memorable.

I remember one joke that resonated with the public took place one Saturday afternoon in Uxbridge Woolworths. As I was leaving the store, a 6 foot tall, 20 stone friend of Frank's came charging through the door, barged into me and knocked me flat on my back. A young girl shop assistant, who I knew well, came up to me and asked if I wanted a hand. I said "Yes", and when she bent down and extended her hands, I grabbed hold of them and pulled her down on top of me and lay there with my legs splayed wide open screaming, "Help!" "Rape!" "Rape!" The girl got up, blushed, and fled.

Another notable prank took place when I was working for the R.S.P.C.A. in the West End of London. One afternoon, after finishing work, I walked to Oxford Circus tube station to catch the train home. It was a beautiful, sunny, midsummer's day, without a cloud in the sky. When I arrived at Notting Hill Gate station, 10 minutes later, it was pouring with rain. I was amazed and mystified – how had the weather changed so suddenly. Frank had water bowsers spraying water over the station's exit.

Also, as a result of my cogitations, I get photos of the crime scene from a Picture Library. The one showing the rear window of the royal car quite clearly displays a large hole where the bullet is supposed to have passed through, completely different to the small star bullet hole depicted in the 'Daily Telegraph' the day after the hoax.

I remember my conversation with Mr Thorpe about Princess Anne, and specifically about the story I had read regarding the hoax involving the Royal Family. The book containing the story was entitled 'Frauds and Hoaxes' and it was in Kensington Library.

It stands to reason that if I can prove the existence of the book it will help my case, so I write to the library and ask them to supply me with a statement confirming they stock the book, which they do.

I also recall that a couple of days before the hoax I had opened an account with Barclays Bank in Watford, and deposited an envelope containing my passport, driving licence, pilot's licence, insurance card, P40 and P60 in the safe.

I, therefore, decide to try and withdraw the £200 I had deposited in the account, and also request the return of the envelope and contents.

However, when I contact the bank, they say they can find no trace of the account or the envelope. Their excuse? The records probably got lost when the bank moved location.

I therefore complain to Barclays Head Office about their incompetence, but they provide no satisfaction, so I write to the Financial Ombudsman. However, the Ombudsman says that as I have no proof that I opened the account, they are unable to help.

Little by little a pattern is emerging – for example, in an effort to establish the correct date, I write to Bow Street Police Station asking for a copy of my 20th March charge sheet. Like my various bank records, it has been destroyed.

In another effort to establish the correct date, I write to the Lebanese Consulate and ask them for a copy of the visa I obtained for a visit to the country in 1973(74). They can apparently find no record of the visa.

In the mid 90s I learn that Police Committees have been set up for each London borough to investigate complaints against the police. I write to each one, complaining about Frank and asking them to make the appropriate enquiries to find him. Several try but are unsuccessful. However, when a member of one of the committees tries to visit me in Broadmoor, he is turned away at the gate.

I therefore write to the Criminal Cases Review Commission asking them to review my case. They say that, as the incident took place a long time ago, it would now be impossible to prove it was a hoax.

During the time I have been incarcerated, the outside world has changed, with one of the biggest changes being the massive growth of the internet.

I realise that this presents a huge opportunity for me to get word out about my case; of the hoax; of my continued imprisonment; and of the steps being taken to block me. I, therefore, decide to put the details of my case on the internet.

I compile a document explaining how the incident was a hoax and how I am an innocent sane man who is being detained purely for his dissenting political philosophies and offer a one-million-pound reward to anyone who proves I am an innocent sane man and gets me out.

I send the document to Knowledge Computing, a website hosting company, and ask them to put it on the internet. However, the letter is intercepted by my RMO, and once more blocked.

I write to the Superintendent, ask him to overrule the RMO, which predictably, he refuses to do.

In response, I send him a stinking letter telling him that I am going to take legal proceedings against him for conspiracy to pervert the course of justice. This involves a lengthy correspondence with the Mental Health Act Commission.

After nine months it appears that I am getting nowhere, so I enlist the help of my solicitor.

She also enters into a lengthy correspondence with the MHAC, and when she too gets nowhere, she decides to make an application for a Judicial Review.

First she gets a Council's opinion. He says I have a good case.

Then it goes before a judge – he says I have a good case.

However, when it goes to court, the judge refuses the application.

I tell my solicitor to launch an appeal, which she does.

We win, so the case goes ahead.

Each side gathers evidence to support their respective cases.

Then their side come up with the suggestion that the proceedings would trigger post-traumatic stress disorder in the victims of the offence, in light of which, my solicitor bows out.

Unwilling to drop the matter at this stage, I decide to act as Litigant In Person, however, I am informed by my RMO that they are going to try to get the judge to rule that the hearing should be private.

This would obviously be of no use to me, as I need this matter to be as public as possible, so I correspond with Reid Minty, the hospital's solicitors, bring to their attention the points of law I can invoke to make sure that they don't get a private hearing.

Eventually they relent, say the hearing will be public, but then point out that for security reasons, I will not be able to attend court.

Again I correspond with Reid Minty, again they relent.

The case proceeds, with me spending untold hours preparing my case, however, about a month before it is due to be heard, the Court writes to inform me that the judge will be coming to Broadmoor to conduct the hearing.

Obviously, this is of no use to me, so I write to the Court pointing out that the Broadmoor authorities have now changed their minds and said that I can attend Court.

The Court is adamant, however, says that this doesn't make any difference and that the hearing must be held in Broadmoor.

As a result of this development, I reluctantly come to the conclusion that there is no point in continuing the case.

Another door has been closed to me.

I inform my RMO that, as the case is no longer going ahead, if the Broadmoor authorities have not given me explicit permission to put the details of my case on the internet by the 1st January 2002, I will refuse my medication and go on hunger strike.

2002 dawns and I have still not received such permission, so I inform my RMO that I am going on hunger strike, effective immediately. The RMO responds in the usual manner by threatening to give me ECT.

I commence my hunger strike.

I have been through this before, so am not surprised when I am transferred to the hospital wing, and immediately on arrival taken to the clinical room to be fitted with a feeding tube.

This procedure ranges from extremely unpleasant through to downright painful.

First there is the sensation of the tube passing near the sinuses as it is pushed through my nose and into my throat, which causes my eyes to water.

Then there is an intense burning and gagging sensation as it goes down my throat.

Finally, when the tube enters the stomach there is a strong urge to vomit.

Once correctly inserted, the tube is attached to a large, domed, liquid food container mounted on top of a long pole. Whenever I move, I have to pull this contraption along – it is like being shadowed by one of Doctor Who's Daleks.

Being on hunger strike is miserable. Not only do I have my own personal Dalek to drag around whenever I want to go anywhere, but I also find that the liquid diet gives me semi-permanent diarrhoea, so that I find myself constantly having to dash to the toilets, my companion clanking along behind me.

In addition, although the feeding tube keeps me from starving, it is not like eating a meal, so I constantly feel hungry, especially at meal times, when the smell of the food, even the lousy hospital food they serve, drives me crazy.

Being on hunger strike also comes with its share of indignity – I am forcibly injected by half a dozen burly screws every two weeks, including some female staff members. After a short while I have a lovely assortment of cuts and bruises from being manhandled, while my pride is just as badly dented from having my arse and ball sack exposed to the world on a regular basis.

Rules are rules, so every month or so, a man from the Mental Health Act Commission comes to see how I am doing, and assures me that he is on the case.

Every 4 or 5 weeks, I write to the Chief Executive. As Broadmoor Special Hospital Authority has combined with several Mental Health NHS Trusts to form West London Mental Health NHS Trust, we now have a Chief Executive in charge instead of a Superintendent.

I have nicknamed her Gertrude. Our correspondence goes something like this:

Me: "There is no difference between the Internet and the newspapers – Broadmoor is 20 years behind the times."

Gertrude: 'Access to the Internet is banned by the Department of Health's Mandatory Directions 1999.'

Me: 'The Directions don't apply. I want to put stuff on, not copy data from the Internet. Anyway, Broadmoor isn't a hospital, it's a prison.'

Gertrude: 'Section 134 applies to all patients detained under the 1983 Mental Health Act.'

Me: 'Only Subsection (1)(a) applies in his case.'

Gertrude: No reply…

Me: 'The reason you haven't replied is because you are too ashamed to admit you are wrong about Section 134 and the Security Directions'.

Gertrude: 'I have nothing further to add on the subject.'

Me: I explain my dissenting philosophies and how Britain is an upper class dictatorship, which she is helping to perpetuate…

Gertrude: 'I suggest you discuss the matter with your RMO.'

Me: 'There is no point in me discussing it with my RMO, because whatever he says carries no weight, as any of his orders can be countermanded by you.'

And then, lo and behold, the MHAC (Mental Health Act

Commission) completes their investigation and finds in my favour!

My conversation with Gertrude finally concludes:

Me: 'I take it that it is now OK for me to put the details of my case on the Internet?'

Gertrude (somehow sounding completely pissed off in a letter): 'The hospital will action the Commission's decision.'

In early 2003, I am finally able to put details of my case on the Internet. However, aware of the fact that simply having it there is no good if people aren't aware of its existence, I try to put an advert in the 'Evening Standard' newspaper, bringing the public's attention to the existence of my website.

I am, of course, prevented from doing so by my RMO, so once again I appeal to the MHAC, once again they find in my favour.

However, when I try to insert the advert in the 'Daily Telegraph', they refuse to accept it because they say it would lay them open to proceedings for libel.

My RMO seizes upon this like a dog with a fresh bone, writes to the MHAC, and, quoting the 'Daily Telegraph', tries to stop me putting future adverts in the newspapers.

I write to the Commission giving a list of reasons why the newspapers would not be sued for libel, and the Commission once more finds in my favour.

I like to think that all of this has really pissed off Gertrude and my RMO, and let's face it, after decades of battles I think I am long overdue a few victories.

After this, I am free to run the advert bringing the public's attention to the existence of my website, and so, over the next three years I write to all the local and national newspapers I can find, asking them to insert the advert. About a quarter agree.

The word is finally getting out there.

Broadening my horizons, I also send it to the 'New York Times', 'New York Post', 'Daily News', 'Los Angeles Times', 'Washington Post' and 'USA Today'. Only 'USA Today' replies and accepts it.

I send the paper $275 to pay for the advert, but the money

is returned with a note saying they are unable to publish it. It seems America is not receptive to me.

Over the course of the next couple of years I have some wins, and some losses:

The publication 'Class War' runs the ad and also suggests I write a column for the paper.

The advert runs in 'Private Eye'.

ITV broadcast a drama/documentary about the affair entitled, 'To kidnap a Princess', almost none of which is factually correct.

'The Guardian' refuses to insert the advert.

My RMO gives me a copy of a letter from the broadcasting company 'Atlas', saying that they are in the process of making a documentary about the affair.

I send the details of my case to the leaders of every foreign country – a total of over 200 – and receive many replies. Not one takes it up with the UK government, however.

I obtain a copy of the Law Society's 'Directory of Solicitors and Barristers' and write to 100 human rights solicitors/barristers explaining my situation and asking them to take action based on the 1998 Human Rights Act, which incorporates the rights set out in the European Convention on Human Rights into domestic British law.

I send letters explaining my situation to ten working-class union bosses, to Reprieve, to The Prison Reform Trust and to NACRO. All refuse to help. It's probably not surprising that NACRO refused, as their patron is the Queen.

I buy Willings Press Guide volumes 1–3 and write to local, regional and national newspapers in every country in the world – over 3,000 letters in all. In my letters I explain how the incident was a hoax and point out that the easiest way they can prove it was a hoax is to check their old newspapers and establish that the event took place in 1975 and not 1974 as the authorities are asserting. This will prove it was a hoax because it means that I was living one year behind everybody else, and the amount of contact Frank and his associates would have had to have to maintain the time deception proves that it would have been impossible for me to plan and execute a real kidnap attempt.

I further point out that if they are the ones to prove it was a hoax, it will really put their newspaper on the map and bring them fame and fortune because it will receive world-wide publicity and they will be feted as heroes.

When I send the letter to the foreign newspapers, I have the first paragraph of the letter translated into the 10 major foreign languages, so they should at least be able to understand the first paragraph if nothing else.

I also offer a £1 million reward which I intend to raise by publishing my autobiography and suing the authorities.

I don't receive replies to any of these letters. I can only conclude that they have been intercepted by Frank, working in tandem with my RMO and the authorities. The fact that they are still so consistently blocking me only strengthens my resolve, makes me more determined than ever to prove my innocence.

Meanwhile, life in Broadmoor continues pretty much as it has. One of the few noticeable changes is that female nurses now work on the male side in secure hospitals. These nurses aren't as you'd expect – built like brick shithouses, with a moustache and hairy legs – but rather, they are young and feminine, and some are even pretty. Some are staff nurses, some ordinary nurses and some health care assistants.

As mentioned previously, there is one who works on my ward called Cynthia, or as the wags like to call her, "Sinful Cyn", who, against all the rules, is rumoured to be having an affair with Dexter, the young handsome alpha male who effectively runs the ward.

It actually suits the screws to have a patient who makes sure everything is running smoothly. Dexter sorts out disputes between patients, organises things such as the ward horse racing sweepstake and the ward parties, even arranges such things as food and drink, an outside disco, or an outside comedian to come in and perform.

"Sinful Cyn" and Dexter seem to be genuinely in love, are frequently seen sitting together, holding hands and talking intimately. The rumour is that they have had sex, a rumour that we are all willing to perpetuate, as sex with "Sinful Cyn" is something that pretty much all the male patients on the ward would sell their souls for. Like most of the other inmates I observe their relationship with envy, wishing I were fifty years younger, or could occupy Dexter's shoes for just one day.

One of the biggest characters on the ward is a tall, athletic Scotsman nicknamed "Jock". Jock has flaming red hair and a volatile temperament to match, loves listening to bagpipe music.

Every few days, Jock marches into the day room with his favourite bagpipe CD in his hand, removes whatever is playing, then inserts his CD, turns the sound system up full blast, and stands in front of the speakers with a huge smile on his face.

On this particular occasion, however, the CD that is currently playing is Dexter's, and he doesn't take too kindly to having his music interrupted, especially as he is sitting canoodling with "Sinful Cyn", the two of them listening to their favourite romantic ballads.

As the sound of the bagpipes fills the room, Dexter jumps up. "Oy! Jockie! We were listening to that."

Jock, seemingly oblivious to Dexter's complaint, continues to stand in front of the speakers, a blissful smile on his face.

Not used to being ignored, Dexter marches up in front of Jock, gets in his face. "Oy. Are you listening to me, you hairy Scottish twat?"

Jock finally deigns to look at him.

What will happen?

Dexter rules the ward with charm and subterfuge, and on the strength of his connections with the screws, but Jock is at least six inches taller than Dexter, and a good four stone heavier. If it comes to a physical encounter, Jock will wipe the floor with him.

"What's the matter, wee man?" asks Jock over the noise of the bagpipes.

"It's this bleeding racket," yells Dexter in response. "It's not even real music!"

Jock looks affronted. "Not real music?"

"Yeah. You can't dance to it or nothing."

Jock stares at him in disbelief. "Can't dance to it?"

"Right."

"The little you know," replies Jock, and immediately begins stripping off his clothes until all that remains is his tartan beret, whereupon he starts dancing a vigorous Scottish reel.

As he starts dancing we are all transfixed at the sight of Jock lurching from side to side, for between his legs dangles the largest set of tackle that any of us has ever seen.

But it is not just the patients who are transfixed – "Sinful Cyn" is also watching, mouth open in disbelief, her eyes affixed to the great thing swinging between his legs, as if mesmerised by a giant hypnotist's watch and chain.

Dexter gazes between Jock and Sinful Cyn for a long moment, unused to losing control of the ward, before finally shouting, "Oy! Cyn! Do something!"

Upon hearing his words, Sinful Cyn reluctantly drags her eyes away from the monstrous appendage, runs into the corridor and shouts, "STAFF!"

Within seconds four screws race into the room, one female staff nurse and three male staff, one of whom has obviously just come in from outside, as he is still wearing his hat.

It takes all five of them to wrestle Jock to the ground, then lead him away, the aforementioned hat now employed to cover Jock's private parts.

Once Jock is escorted out and put in isolation, Sinful Cyn returns, slumps into an armchair, gazes into space.

Dexter stares at her blankly, can't think of anything to say.

Chalk that one up as a win for Jock, I think, trying not to laugh out loud.

Chapter 24

I had always thought that Voodoo was a myth, hadn't realised that it was a real thing, and that the Voodoo religion is taken seriously by millions of people, until I read an article in the Sunday paper. It explained that Voodoo is the dominant religion in Haiti, and that over two million people in America practise the Voodoo religion.

I find this of great interest because, for the past thirty years, I have been getting tremendous pains all over my body. It is excruciating, feels like someone is sticking red hot needles into my body, and at times has me rolling around on the floor in agony.

If the Voodoo religion is a reality, I think, it means that Voodoo Dolls are also a reality, in which case, could Frank have made an effigy of me, into which he regularly sticks pins?

Having read the article, I now consider this not to be beyond the bounds of possibility.

Thinking back, I recall that the pains started about twenty years after I was confined in hospital. This would be the time when it had become obvious to the authorities that the normal torture regime of drugs, electric shocks (ECT), etc, were having no effect, and weren't going to break me, so Frank could have decided to try psychic torture.

Not that they don't still use the traditional methods. One of the main techniques, which I have experienced throughout my stay in both Rampton and Broadmoor, is forcible injections. At Broadmoor, this is compounded by the presence of female screws. Having your trousers and pants yanked down to expose your private parts while women stand there with pleasurable grins on their faces is truly one of the most humiliating experiences possible.

Over the years I have developed a theory as to why they get so much pleasure out of it. I believe it is because women are usually the ones in the vulnerable position, being humiliated, so when the tables are turned and it is the man undergoing the same treatment, the females get a great deal of pleasure out of it.

Another newspaper article that I read around this time gets me thinking. It reports that the British Government has condemned the Chinese Government for incarcerating political dissenters, for having political prisoners.

I think this is a bit rich, like the pot calling the kettle black, because it was quite common for the British Government to incarcerate political dissenters in the late '60's and early '70's.

Apart from me, there were several other political prisoners being held during my time in Rampton. One patient had been convicted of shoplifting and had been detained for twenty years just because he was critical of the Rampton regime.

Another patient, who I used to call One-Eyed-Pete (because he only had one eye and his name was Peter!), had been locked up for eight years for a minor burglary for which he would normally have served just one year.

He too was critical of the Rampton regime, and had reported several screws to the police for violent and abusive behaviour. The response? The police just gave the screws more time to work on him, beating him up, increasing his medication, and giving him ECT, until he was forced to withdraw his complaint.

Although Pete was too scared to give practical support for my campaign to get a public enquiry into Rampton, he did provide moral support. I was particularly fond of him because he was a humanitarian and was always doing things to help the patients. He even learnt sign language so that he could communicate with a deaf and dumb patient.

In support of my own claim to be a political prisoner, I had pointed out to RMO Hazzard on several occasions that I was detained in a State Psychiatric Institution (Rampton was directly funded and controlled by the Ministry of Health), by a State Psychiatrist (Hazzard) and had been driven to the institution by the State Police (Frank was a member of the Metropolitan Police and the Met was directly financed and controlled by the Home Office. Special Branch was part of the Metropolitan Police and it dealt with domestic political dissenters, such as myself).

In fact, I have been subjected to harassment due to my political beliefs ever since I was first arrested.

As a result, I conclude that I should be able to apply to the High Court for a Restraining Order. I, therefore, write to a solicitor asking him if I can apply for the Order and if so, how much it will cost. The answer is in the affirmative and the quoted cost is £10,000.

I see my Responsible Clinician (the new name for RMOs) and inform him that I am thinking of applying for a Restraining Order. I also remind him of the existence of my website and of all the letters I have sent, in order to convince him that my case has already received so much exposure that there is now no point in him preventing me from publishing my autobiography.

The RC has a long think and then, to my utter amazement, says, "Yes. OK."

I am ecstatic! I have finally achieved my objective and will now be getting out.

Why do I think that? Because a lot of people, including the people in The Mall on the night of the incident, know it was a hoax, and when they read my autobiography and find out that I know it was a hoax and that I am not happy, it will be clear that my detention isn't helping me, and they will want to get me out.

The other thing that excites me is that once I am out I will take steps to activate my psychic powers. Hazzard had told me that the best way I can do this is by building up my self-confidence, by making love to beautiful women.

How will I find these women? My plan is to do so by asking,

in my autobiography, for them to contact me. I am certain that there will be plenty of women willing to accommodate me because, not only will they be helping me, but they will also be benefiting themselves, as making love to me will result in me turning their bodies back so that they remain young and beautiful and live forever, with an IQ of 160 and a photographic memory.

And of course once I activate my ESP powers I will turn my own body back, allowing me to achieve an overwhelming victory in my long-standing war, because not only will I be free, but over time I will remain alive while all my enemies will die of old age.

There is just one thing wrong with my plan. After the affair has been made public I will be famous and will receive attention from the world's Press, which will hamper my efforts to associate with beautiful women.

I would be a lot happier if there was a way I could associate with the women without publishing my autobiography, but women are obviously not going to believe me when I say I can turn their bodies back, I will have to have some form of proof.

After much consideration I conclude that one highly effective form of proof would be an official document signed by the Queen stating that I have ESP and can turn women's bodies back. If such a document were created it would not only benefit me, it would also benefit the Queen, because, if she were to sign the document, it would prove that she has been hoodwinked by Frank's associates, but is now sorry that she has unwittingly helped them to detain me for all these years. In this case, I would not be critical of Her Majesty and would not want her to be prosecuted and sent to prison.

However, if she refuses to sign, it will prove that she is willingly and actively persecuting and silencing me because I am a threat to her luxurious way of living. In fact, she is the ring leader. In this case, I would inflame public opinion and have her stripped of her immunity from prosecution. I would then make sure she was prosecuted and sentenced to spend the rest of her natural life in prison.

However, it is possible that the Queen might have a valid reason for not signing the document. She might believe Frank and his associates when they say I am too weak and inadequate to get an erection, and therefore won't be able to make love to the beautiful women. However, although the torture has severely weakened me, I am still confident that I will be able to perform when required, and anyway, even if I can't, I can always take Viagra. At the moment, I admire and respect the Queen, so I don't want to sue or prosecute her, but I will if I have to.

Reflecting on my time in Rampton and Broadmoor, I feel that the time hasn't been completely wasted, because my various campaigns have resulted in the total transformation of society. Whereas in the past, the upper class were the preferred class, nowadays the working class are preferred, and everybody tries to make out they are from this social group, including the upper class. Being the architect of such a transformation is truly gratifying. Some of the campaigns I have initiated and the results I have achieved are:

(1) To improve the life of the patients and of the members of the general public by setting up a Public Enquiry into the screws' brutality at Rampton.

Not only would this improve the patients' lives, it would also benefit society in general, because the better treatment the patients would receive after the enquiry would improve their mental condition and make it less likely that they would commit further offences.

As a result of my efforts, such an enquiry has taken place.

(2) To improve people's faith in the fairness of the legal processes by establishing fair, impartial Mental Health Review Tribunals, and giving them the power to discharge the patients.

The Tribunals now have this power thanks to my European Court application.

(3) To improve the quality of life of people living with a mental illness by giving them greater rights. To this end, I proposed a new, improved, Mental Health Act to replace the monstrously outdated 1959 Act.

We now have the 1983 Mental Health Act.

(4) To improve the human rights of every citizen by ensuring that the Government treats everyone equally, with fairness, dignity, and respect. This should be accomplished by incorporating the rights set out in the European Convention on Human Rights into domestic British law. Then, when someone considered that their human rights had been breached, they could seek a remedy in the British courts rather than pursuing a time consuming and costly remedy in the European Court of Human Rights.

We now have the 1998 Human Rights Act.

(5) To improve the life of people accused of a crime and remanded in custody. For example, someone accused of a minor crime such as shoplifting could spend anything up to two years on remand. If they were then found not guilty, it would mean that an innocent person had spent two years in prison.

This has now been rectified.

(6) To improve life of each and every citizen by making it much less likely that they become the victim of a miscarriage of justice.

I had therefore proposed that the police should be restricted to gathering the evidence relating to a crime, and should have no say in whether or not the suspect should be prosecuted. After completing their enquiries, the police should hand over the evidence to a separate, independent, body to decide if any charges should be brought. That would help prevent miscarriages of justice such as the I one experienced.

We now have the Crown Prosecution Service to serve this function.

(7) To improve the life of millions of workers and prevent them from being exploited by their upper-class bosses, by imposing a statutory minimum wage.

This has now been implemented.

(8) To improve the life of employees by passing a law banning discrimination on the grounds of political beliefs, religious beliefs, disability, race, marriage, age, gender or sex.

Such a law has now been passed.

(9) To improve the life of tenants by setting up a tribunal that a tenant can go to and give evidence in person if they think they have been unfairly evicted or their rent is too high.

This is now in place.

(10) To improve the life of working class schoolchildren by improving the educational system to such an extent that, instead of just a select few pupils going to university, all children have the opportunity to do so.

Now, half of all schoolchildren go to university.

How much my campaigns have contributed to the improvements that have been made will not be known until the affair is made public. However, once the matter is public knowledge, the various Prime Ministers will have to say that my contributions have been significant because, although they have been keeping me locked up to silence me, they will now have to say that they have been trying to help me, and that part of that help was to humour me by taking notice of my various campaigns.

Perhaps in recognition of this, and the simple fact that you can't keep the truth bottled up forever, I receive a visit from a Mister Davis (name changed to protect the guilty!) from the Ministry of Justice.

We are shown to a small, private room by one of the screws, and once the door is closed, Mister Davis, a grey man in a grey suit, carefully explains that if I were to sign a statement saying I would not sue nor seek to prosecute those involved in my detention, the authorities will release me and pay me a £1million settlement. He also makes it quite clear that on no account will I be able to publish my autobiography, and I will also have to sign a gagging order to that effect.

Once he has finished, Davis leans forward eagerly, licks his lips. "Shall I show you the documents?" he says, "then you can sign them."

I sit tight, mull over his proposition.

My first response is pure excitement. I could soon be out, a free man, with a million pounds in the bank. What more could I want?

The answer comes to me quickly.

The truth.

Recognition.

Respect.

I lean forward.

Davis' hand is twitching, reaching for his briefcase, ready to flourish the papers at me, secure my signature, silence me.

I let him sweat for a moment longer, then quickly stand up.

Davis flinches as though I am about to hit him, but I head

straight for the door, where I pause, one hand on the door handle.
"You have the papers with you, right now?"

He nods eagerly, like a dog about to receive a treat.

"Then I suggest you take them and…"

I don't finish the sentence, march out, my head held high.

They thought I was weak.

They thought I would cave in.

They were wrong.

I am clear in my mind what I need to do.

I need to stay true to my beliefs, have faith in my campaigns, and publish my autobiography. Once it is out in the public domain, the genie will truly be out of the bottle, and no matter what the Prime Minister says, I am confident that I will be able to prove that I have been consistently persecuted and tortured. As a result, when I sue the authorities I should get a small fortune in damages. I will also get a significant amount from the sales of my autobiography, because it will be a bestseller.

So, not only will I be associating with beautiful women, I will also be able to afford to buy my dream car, a Ferrari, an aerobatic light aircraft, and a yacht. I will also be able to go on exotic holidays, and indulge my passions of the theatre and the cinema by going every week.

Life is looking rosy!

Afterword

Are you a budding Hercule Poirot or Miss Marple. If you are, you can earn £1,000.

I am in the process of writing the 2nd edition and it would help if I knew a way the protagonist can prove that the hoax kidnap took place on the 20th March 1975 and not the 20th March 1974. I can't think of a way. If you can, I will give you £1,000.

It shouldn't just be something that the protagonist can prove to himself as he has already said he can do this by getting the weather forecasts. It should be something the protagonist can show to other people to prove it.

You have to remember that Frank is a very resourceful individual so if, for example, the protagonist were to try and get a foreign newspaper for the appropriate day in 1975, Frank could just nobble the newspaper's publisher and get them to print a fake copy of their paper. Or Frank could make up and print a copy himself.

It's a knotty problem and anybody who solves it deserves the £1,000.

Write to: Ian Ball, PO Box 79032, London, W2 7GY.

www.ingramcontent.com/pod-product-compliance
Lightning Source LLC
Chambersburg PA
CBHW070359200726
48294CB00003B/1000